Big Kiwi
Suspense Under the Southern Cross

Reggie Brick

Reggie Brick Books

Contents

Dedication

Dedicated to . . .
My husband and favorite pilot who inspired the best parts of
Neve;
and to
Don, Susan, Chris, Jay, Julie, Carol, Savannah and Alexis who
contributed to the story's authenticity.

Chapter 1

Swan Dive

Logan - Jenae

Sheets of rain blinded a "dead man" on the run. Red lights ahead of him glowed brighter and then dimmer as traffic moved forward on a Northern California highway. Logan kept an eye on his wristwatch and squinted forward to see through the heavy downpour, while he navigated stop and go traffic. An Air Force base was forty miles away, and he had fifty-three minutes before a large transport plane was scheduled to depart for the Philippines. His right hand rested on a black duffle bag with his most important possessions – twenty grand in cash, black and red basketball shoes, a concert T-shirt, shorts, gummy candies and a revolver. Tucked inside his black and red basketball shoes was an extra-large box of medium size ribbed condoms.

His buddy, Bart, made the clandestine stowaway exit from the U.S. possible. Bart really wasn't his buddy, but just another acquaintance who owed Logan a huge debt, and this was the final payment. Blackmail was the most efficient way Logan got things done.

Bart's words on the phone (before Logan jacked a car parked on Eddy Street in the Fillmore District, played on a loop in his mind). "This is it. If you don't make my flight and get your butt into the cargo hold, our books are still cleared. I owe you nothing. In fact, if you show your pathetic dome again, I'll expose that you faked your own suicide on Christmas Eve by leaving your shoes and wallet on the Golden Gate Bridge."

Thoughts of successfully pulling off his own suicide made his ingenious escape plan from the United States even more glorious. He had to do it to avoid his own agency from court marshaling him. A fresh start was crucial for redemption. Offenses that the FBI had against him were numerous and egregious, and the last one landed him in the hospital for a few weeks with a cracked skull. The FBI was willing to prosecute one of their own even though Logan had gone above and beyond his duties. *I can't believe they would turn on me after everything I've done for those bastards.*

Jenae was his ultimate downfall – the nurse that he'd been in love with over a year had betrayed him. His plan to disrupt her true love for a New Zealander was thwarted when he confessed his diabolical obsession for her.

His sexual stalking of Jenae started during a FBI work-related stakeout in Hawaii and continued on the mainland. Unbeknownst to Logan, Jenae said "yes" to the Kiwi on Christmas Eve on the same night that Logan faked his own suicide. Behind the scenes scheming kept Neve from staying in the United States, but Jenae swerved around Logan's evil endeavors. She planned to live in New Zealand with Neve until his immigration status could be worked out. As far as she knew, Logan was still dead.

Heavy rain abated and phantom Logan made up time when the highway cleared. The base was in his sights and he knew a shortcut to the airfield where a C-141 was almost finished loading. Bart finished an initial cockpit checklist and walked around the plane, inspected the tires and checked the integrity of the aircraft. At the same time, he scanned the fence line looking for Logan to meet him at the back gate. *I hope this SOB doesn't make it . . . I wish he really would've jumped off the Golden Gate Bridge. My life would have been so much easier. I bet a whole lot of people would've been better off without his threats to ruin their lives. He collected videos of so many guys that he worked with. Sure, we were doing stuff that we weren't supposed to, but to blackmail us with that shit? He doesn't give a damn about our lives now, most of us have wives and children and he wants to ruin that for us? He's nuts. Screw him. I want to drop him off in the jungles of the Philippines and never see his sorry ass again.*

The fence line was clear, for as much as Bart could see at 2145 on a humid night. No headlights, only a concert of locusts chirped in the trees nearby and the smell of jet fuel hung in the air from the tanker truck nearby. Airmen loaded final crates of cargo with a pulley system through a back hatch of the C-141 and secured them with anchors and nets. The last airman saluted Bart as he left the cargo area. "All loaded up, Sir." Captain Bart saluted him back.

Logan raced through a wooded thicket and lost a shoe in the process. He stepped on a thorn bush and as he limped to the fence line he caught a glimpse of Captain Bart in his green jumpsuit checking a hatch on the right side of the plane. "Psst...psst," Logan sounded, but couldn't be heard amongst the symphony of insects. Bart turned in front of the plane for a final inspection. Logan screamed in desperation, "BAAART! BAAART! I'm here!" He waited for Bart to appear, "BAAART!"

Halfway up the stairway, Captain Bart stopped to listen. He heard a cry in the humid wind, "BAAART, don't leave me!" Bart dropped his chin to his chest and let out a heavy sigh as he turned and jogged back down the stairs. He saluted the airman on the tarmac and told him to hold for a few more minutes to check something out. He opened a hatch before walking quickly to the gate on the fence line. Logan was crouched under a bush and popped up as Bart approached.

"Thank you! Thank you! I will never bother you again if you deliver me to the Philippines," Logan pleaded.

"I'll go through with it on two conditions. You will never threaten another human being again. And you will never return to the United States of America." Bart poked his finger into the chest of Logan's sweaty shirt.

"I promise. I swear! I've got no other options. I'll never come back and never threaten anyone ever again. I'll walk the straight and narrow from now on. I swear on my mom's life."

Bart swiftly walked Logan to the opened hatch on the plane and helped push him up metal rod stairs. "I better not hear a peep from you this whole trip. I'll check on you once, but that's it." He secured the hatch behind him and jogged through rain puddles on the tarmac to the other side of the plane to board and finalize paperwork. As Bart settled into his seat, wiped his brow, and clipped his seat belts, his first officer turned his head to the left and said, "is everything all right?"

"Everything's just perfect." Bart rolled his eyes and sighed.

⁓⁓◆⁓⁓

Graduation ceremony under bluebird skies was surreal but also a little bit sad for Jenae. Not one family member showed up to celebrate her highest level of educational achievement – Master in Business Administration. She had a smidge of regret for not inviting anyone to the big occasion, only because she decided to walk for graduation at the last minute. It felt right for her as an introvert with extrovert social skills. Classmates convinced her to get her name on the roster to receive her diploma in person, because they knew they wouldn't see each other again anytime soon. A recent grad lent her an official black robe and green and gold sash regalia for the event, but

Jenae had to beg an officiant for a yellow tassel adorned by a gold colored '90 ornament.

A cool breeze dried up tears that welled in her eyes as a friend and classmate gave a heartwarming speech before her class was called to walk across the stage. As Jenae solemnly approached the steps, she handed a card with her name phonetically spelled out to a professor holding a microphone. It was her given name at birth and she wondered if it would be the last time she would hear it aloud.

The five months since her engagement to Neve had flown by in her frenzy to finish business school with an overloaded schedule. Neve had wanted to get married as soon as she arrived in New Zealand, but it was a scary proposition for her to marry and move so far away. Her two previous visits to the land down under were magical, but Jenae had never lived outside of the U.S. Worst of all, her mother strongly disapproved; not of the marriage, but of Jenae moving to another hemisphere.

Changing her difficult last name to Neve's was a positive move in her mind. For her entire life, most people didn't spell or say it correctly. She hoped that she wouldn't cringe when the announcer read her card. *Amazing! She said it right,* Jenae thought as she smiled and gave a little wave to cheering friends sitting in folding chairs on the lawn below her. She shook the Dean's hand who handed her a leather diploma holder embossed with the university's golden emblem. The president reached out his hand as she tripped over a microphone cord that came loose on stage. He caught her from falling and her cheek landed on his shoulder as a few gasps escaped from the student section. With a reddened face she turned to the audience again and held her diploma above her head with unconvincing bravado.

The climax of the ceremony signified a new beginning in her life. Her cap thrown in the air with all of her classmates, reminded her of how far she had come since the last time she tossed it at her nursing school graduation. Working as a registered nurse in hospitals in Texas and Hawaii seemed like a big adventure. But getting married to the love of her life and moving to New Zealand was even bigger. The stalker who terrorized her over the past year was dead, and life was good again.

"Hey Jenae, come get a group photo with us on stage!" Her squad waved her over.

"Sure, let me find my cap. It's under one of these chairs."

As Jenae laughed with her classmates, a man from the shadows of a nearby cedar tree held a program in front of his face and sauntered through white wooden chairs. A Giants baseball cap and black sunglasses matched his black jacket and pants. He slowly walked off campus toward manicured lawns in the adjacent neighborhood, while Jenae mugged for cameras. "Say CHEESE!"

Hugs and goodbyes finished off the ceremony, which signified the ending of some of the best two years of her life. Jenae thought of all of the unceremonious chores she had to tend to before she left the country. Her best friend invited her for a meal with her family at the country club later that day, but Jenae politely declined. Picture-taking was a fun distraction and she almost forgot about her favorite sweater neatly folded on the seat of her chair. It was her deceased grandmother's knitted handiwork. As she picked it up, a card slipped out and fell on freshly cut grass below. It read, "Congratulations Jenae." *Huh, I wonder who gave me this. Now I feel like a heel. I didn't get any of my friends cards.*

With her arms full of bunched up graduation garments, Jenae stopped at a bench along the sidewalk to reorganize. The card beckoned her to open it. On the front was a caricature of a white swan with a mortar board on its head, spectacles on its beak and a scroll in its wing. As she read the message on the inside, Jenae jumped up from the bench and screeched. The card flew out of her hands into a rose bush while she crossed her arms across her chest and jumped up and down in fright. Inside, block letters from a black felt tip marker read, "Congratulations Jenae. You are a beautiful swan. I'll be watching over you. Your friend from a watery grave, Logan."

Chapter 2

Best Laid Plans

Jenae - Neve

A whirlwind had swirled in Jenae's brain the month before graduation. Studying for finals was a cakewalk compared to the challenge of completing her master thesis. Waiting on books and documents to arrive at the campus library created a big delay in crafting her work in international market capture. Juggling twelve hour shifts at the hospital and volunteering with the church's senior outreach program didn't help the timeline for finishing her thesis. The thoughts of moving to New Zealand and getting married occupied a whole different bucket in her brain. Compartmentalization was a skill Jenae had mastered as a nurse.

"How many points do I need for a one-way ticket to Auckland, New Zealand?" Jenae held the receiver between her ear and shoulder with a cricked neck at a payphone booth in the hospital lobby.

While the travel agent checked for the best deal, Jenae flipped through her frequent flier cards and shoved them back into her wallet. She had lots of points saved up from her previous journeys to visit Neve in New Zealand that year.

"OK, that sounds perfect. Can you book me the flight all the way to Christchurch? No, I just need a one-way ticket for now. I'm not sure when I'm returning."

"Much appreciated. You have a good day too."

<hr>

A shopping trip to Nordstrom's in Union Square was a must because she wanted to buy the latest Tahari navy suit that she saw advertised in a catalog. She was in desperate need of professional clothing for her anticipated bigwig job in New Zealand. Jenae had made it through business school with cute dresses and blazers, but couldn't justify the cost of a well-made suit until now. She had paid off her credit cards by working extra shifts at the hospital, and saved the insurance money she got from when her car got totaled the year before. She was debt free from business school because of her scholarship. And her grocery bill was minimal because she barely ate to maintain her slender physique.

The heavy glass front door of the department store opened with great effort and Jenae was immediately greeted by a well-dressed woman with perfect red lipstick and a small glass spray bottle. "Would you like to try our newest fragrance? Here, give me your wrist." Jenae gladly pulled up her sleeve and gracefully stretched out her arm presenting the palest part of her upper body. She waited while the fancy lady fanned the fragrance with a promotional card.

"OK, smell it now. Always wait for perfume to dry on your skin to allow the scent to work with your body chemistry."

"Mm, yeah that smells nice. I like it." Jenae smiled and quickly walked toward the escalator knowing that she couldn't afford pricey eau-de-toilet. Some women feel sexy when they walk into a lingerie store, but Jenae felt powerful and sexy when she saw mannequins dressed in designer suits with their fingers rotated pointing to the sky. The professional women's department was empty and a lone stylist was more than happy to pluck garments for her to try on. Jenae wandered around suit racks and found the exact Tahari number that she was looking for. She also found five other skirt suits to try on, along with white and baby-blue professional blouses.

The navy Tahari skirt suit was a must and she picked up another military green colored suit by a well-known designer on sale. Nordstrom was known for having the best shoes in town and Jenae found two pairs of comfortable pumps to go with her new outfits. On the way to the pantyhose department, she passed by another fancy perfume lady.

"No thanks, I already have a scent on my arm," Jenae quietly mouthed and signaled with her hands as she approached.

"Oh, but darling, we just got this fragrance in. Let me show you how to do it." She sprayed in front of her bosom and walked through it like a runway model before turning around with verve and a look that Jenae couldn't deny.

"That looks like fun. Sure, I'll try it," Jenae said before she walked into the suspended spritz and wriggled around in a circle. She smiled with a shopper's high, "I'll take it."

Frugalness and a low maintenance lifestyle had kept Jenae moving in the direction of achieving the life that she dreamed about. But splurging on designer suits and fancy perfume signaled that she was ready to launch into her big life. At the top of her requirements for that life was love, authenticity, a great job, and travel.

⚬

Christchurch, New Zealand was the opposite of a big life in Neve's mind. He had tried to find ways to get to the United States to escape the small island country, but failed at first. Meeting Jenae in Hawaii on vacation felt like a blessing because he truly fell in love with this girl from the middle of America. His heart had been broken three years before by his only other heartthrob from college. When Jenae moved to San Francisco to be with Neve last year, his emotions overflowed. Time was cut short when his U.S. visa extension was denied. He could have married her then to stay in the country, but he wanted to do it right and have all of the pieces of the puzzle in place for a successful life together. Aviation was a big part of that plan, and he had a long way to go starting from zero.

Neve scheduled his first instrument check ride in a Cessna 182 after nine months of grueling flight school. His dream of being a commercial pilot would allow him to live a big life with Jenae and travel the world. The instructor pilot assigned to his check ride made his way to the briefing room where Neve was already waiting, drinking hot tea in a white, foam cup.

The instructor's neatly pressed creased blue trousers with a tight white polo shirt matched the seriousness of his tight buzzed haircut. Neve's wind-blown locks covered his ears and the only clean shirt he could find that morning was a blue floral short-sleeved Hawaiian number. He tucked it into his faded and slightly frayed jeans with a leather belt that emphasized his athletic waistline.

"Did you dress up to impress me, flyboy?" the instructor asked Neve.

"I'm sorry, can you repeat that?" Neve responded.

"Ah, nothing. Heads up . . . if you want to be a commercial pilot, you need to look the part. Get a haircut, son."

"Yes, sir. I guess I screwed up. I'll fix that."

Neve briefed his flight plan aloud while the instructor marked boxes on a checklist. The instructor looked at his watch and motioned toward the door in the side of the hangar as he tightened a baseball cap on his head with the clipboard held under his armpit.

They walked in synchrony onto the tarmac while the instructor peppered him with last minute questions about preflight procedures and weather conditions. Neve felt anxiety build inside of him that made his heart beat faster, and his brain fill with fog.

He had the holding entry rules burned into his brain.

"Sir, holding airspeed for less than 6,000 feet is 200 knots, between 6,000 to 14,000 feet is 230 knots, and above 14,000 feet is 265 knots," Neve enunciated.

"OK son, you prepare the plane and do the walk-around while I watch and listen to your explanations about what you are looking for and thinking about."

"Copy that, sir."

"I will only give you direction once we are airborne and will continue to observe from the right seat."

Neve correctly identified METAR codes for weather conditions . . . FU for smoke, BR for mist, GR for hail, – RA for light rain and + RA for heavy rain. Before take-off, he sat side by side with the instructor in the cockpit, and identified the requirements to continue a landing when conditions were bad.

On the tarmac, Neve sat in the left seat and taxied to the runway, and prepared to perform an instrument departure. He had clearance to point KIWII, which was a point in space 45 miles northeast of the Christchurch VOR on its 060 radial, or path. Once he got there the evaluator asked him to do a series of 45 and 60 degree steep turns to the right and left, and then some "Vertical S" maneuvers where he expertly kept the airplane climbing and then descending at 1000 feet per minute while maintaining the aircraft in 30 degree banked turns to the left and right. Neve was zoned in and his arms were relaxed but strong . . . he made the maneuvers with ease.

"Fly to the 150 radial at 45 DME fix, (another point moored to the southeast of Christchurch) and hold to the southeast of the fix as published using right turns and ten-mile legs," the evaluator instructed.

In past flights, Neve stressed about holding patterns because of the different rules for how aircraft enter depending on where the aircraft enters from. He had to fly the aircraft to the point, set up for the instrument approach that would ensure he maneuvered the aircraft in the correct direction to enter the holding pattern.

Bad dreams about holding patterns had plagued Neve for the past week, but he thought he had conquered the sequence. The mental pressure of the check ride made the events move too fast for his brain to comprehend and Neve succumbed to the dreaded tunnel vision and loss of situational awareness. Instead of turning the aircraft left to parallel the outbound leg of the hold, Neve chose to turn right. The evaluator was forced to take control of the aircraft and put it in the correct position.

Neve's ears roared with the sound of his blood pumping in his head, and both he and the instructor became aware of the pungent aroma wafting from his soaked armpits. He felt dizzy until oxygen until deep, slow breaths forced oxygen into his lungs and brain.

"Are you all right to take over the aircraft, again?" the instructor asked Neve.

"Affirmative, sir," Neve responded with confidence.

The rest of the seventy-minute flight was flawless.

"Your arcs on the touch and go approaches are impressive. Let's set this mother down," said the instructor.

Neve pointed out the fixed distance markers in feet (500, 1,000, 1,500, 2,000, 2,500) on approach. His landing was nearly perfect in the first third of the runway as he described runway identifier lights, PAPI/VASI lights, approach/runway edge/runway center, and touchdown zone lighting to the instructor.

The walk to the debriefing room was too loud to talk because of noise from trucks and planes passing by. The instructor gathered his thoughts on his student's performance, and Neve prepared himself for the worst.

"Son, I'm impressed by your flying knowledge and your overall handling of the plane. Your takeoff and landing were without incident. How do you think you did?" the instructor asked Neve.

"Well sir, I think my nine months of hard work and dedication in preparation for this moment showed. However, the fact that you had to take over the controls on the holding pattern revealed that the stress of the check ride got the best of me," Neve replied.

"If it makes you feel any better, this is a common mistake that new pilots make, maybe because of anxiety related to the evaluation. I'm sorry to inform you that you automatically failed the check ride when I had to take over the controls."

"Can you repeat that?" Neve asked.

"You failed your first check ride. Everything else was perfect and I have no doubt that you will pass it next time. Confidence will come over time with practice."

"Thank you, sir. I wish the result could have been different because I'm committed to flying. You'll hear from me again soon," Neve said with his chin up as he stood to shake hands.

Neve's gut churned as he gathered up his paperwork. He steadied himself on the back of the chair as the instructor let the red metal door slam behind him. Neve felt a waft from the hollow bang as if it kicked him in the pants. He dropped to the floor in a deep squat with his hands clinging to the chair as his chin rested on his chest. Luckily none of his flying mates were milling around to rib him about screwing up, but one of his instructors caught up with him in the parking lot.

"Hey Neve, how'd it go? Did you pass? I bet you passed on the first go around. Am I right?"

"Yeah, not this time mate. I fucked up the holding pattern. I don't know what's wrong with me," Neve mumbled with his hands jammed in his armpits.

"Ah no, I can't believe that. You've been doing so well on our flights."

"I know, you are so calm and relaxed, I think I was missing your energy. That guy was zipped up tight and he made me nervous, you know?" Neve said.

"Don't let it get you down, mate. I'll tell you a secret . . . I didn't pass my first check ride either. But you'll get it the next time. I'll work with you to make sure you do. You need to look through this roadblock, not at it. There is a path to success."

"Thanks man. I really appreciate your support, that means a lot to me." Neve said.

"No worries. I believe in you. Now go relax and have a beer."

Neve was hesitant to tell his family about his failed check ride, but he knew his mum and brother would be supportive no matter what. The thought of telling Jenae was painful. He didn't want to disappoint her because he was learning to fly for the both of them – for their future family. She had too much on her plate and would arrive within the month anyway. She'd be more empathetic and feel comfortable once she was unpacked and back in his arms.

Chapter 3

Equalizing the Past

Jenae - Neve

In the backseat of a large blue Bonneville station wagon, five siblings were packed in shoulder to shoulder, wearing cloth blindfolds. The family vehicle was quiet except for a low volume symphony radiating from the car speakers. While children tried to assess where the beat-up barge of a car was going next, a large bald man driving barked out questions,

"Which way did we turn?

"Left," said Jenae.

"What road are we on?"

"It feels like gravel, it must be the shortcut, Rutan Street," her sister piped up.

"Good job, kids. We're almost home. You can take a look around and see if you were right," their father said.

"Aw Dad, that was too easy. You could have taken us in circles through another neighborhood to make it more challenging."

Jenae's psychiatrist father was always experimenting on his large brood of children. The long hours that he worked meant that his wife had the responsibility of taking care of their six children and household ninety-five percent of the time. Money was always tight feeding eight mouths, and Mom adapted by cutting coupons and assigning hefty chores to the children. Jenae and her sister did laundry, set and cleared the table every night for dinner, loaded the dishwasher and swept the kitchen and dining room. The boys took out the trash and mowed their three-acre lawn in the summertime. Their father chose summer projects for the boys. The biggest was turning an enclosed porch into a bedroom for the two oldest boys. At ages 12 and 13, he gave the boys two hammers and a frugal budget and told them to get to work. No permits were pulled and the boys got to pick out the interiors . . . red and black shag carpet with white walls. Niles decorated with his stash of glow-in-the-dark posters from the local paraphernalia store at the mall. An eight-track stereo was set up on Niles's desk with a black light hanging overhead where he often blasted Lynyrd Skynyrd when his roommate/brother left to study at the library.

It wasn't an accident that long hot summers were filled with full days of activities for six children. Mom wanted the kids out of the house making sure they were too tired to squabble when they returned for dinner and rest. Riding bikes to swim team practice twice before noon each day was half the battle.

"Jenae, sit on top of a towel on the bike rack. Twin, get on the handlebar and put your feet on the nuts on the front wheel." It was easiest to call the youngest "Twin" because they were too identical to get their names correct on the first try. Jenae's oldest brother coordinated a balancing act before pedaling the trio one and a half miles to the city pool. He tried to keep up with the other neighborhood kids but his growing, spindly thirteen-year-old legs didn't have enough power. And the sun rising directly in his eyes made him wobble more.

"Hey! Wait for us," Twin cried ahead.

"We'll patch your tire this afternoon," Brother told Jenae. He was used to hauling one extra person on his bike, but two was too much.

━━━◄O►━━━

Jenae didn't know any other way than to play all day with her friends and siblings. When she wasn't at the community pool, she played kickball, or baseball, or football, or basketball, or shot BB guns, or played in the creek, or made up games that would accommodate all ages of the neighbor kids. On rainy days, they sat in a clearing on the carpet for hours playing board games. Monopoly was the most brutal, not only because of its length, but because her brother, Niles, was known for stealing from the bank when players weren't looking. Her family lived on a quiet, tree-lined street where four prominent doctors, one lawyer, a jeweler, a teacher, an amusement park owner, and a widow owned custom-built homes. The reclusive widow unfortunately looked like the wicked witch of the east as she stood on the back porch and scowled at the children for getting too close to her flower beds and fruit trees.

Jenae started babysitting at age eleven as back up for when her older sister had plans. She loved children and jumped at every chance she got to make extra money. Fifty cents an hour added up and meant she could ride her bike to the local convenience store and buy her own slushy and penny candy anytime she wanted.

She didn't scare easily except when she babysat into the wee hours of the morning at the architect's house. He and his wife were socially mobile and attended the chicest parties in town. The modern home matched their personal style with floor to ceiling windows, which provided no privacy from the woods and creek in the backyard. After their two young children were asleep in their rooms, Jenae's habit was to hide under a blanket on the living room couch, watch TV on low volume and pray to God that the sounds outside the sliding glass doors were only branches blowing in the wind. She felt her chest tighten when she looked at the clock and it struck another hour past midnight. She dozed until a static black and white target took over the TV airwaves at 1 AM and woke her with a high pitch tone. Flipping through the same two table magazines made her yearn for unconsciousness in her own bed. She wanted to be responsible and stay awake until the parents came home, but her usual bedtime was 10 PM on weekends. Her eyes burned between dozing and peeking over the couch through the sliding glass door, to see if a mass murderer was outside, lurking in the stand of elmwood trees behind her.

Physical conditioning and coordination built up by everyday play made competing in school sports easy when the effects of Title IX hit Jenae's middle school. America's constitutional amendment changed her identity. Prior to that, girls sports were limited by economics for the school. High school was the first-time girls' sporting teams were equally funded. Jenae tried out for all of the sports offered, except for golf. Although her lofty height suited volleyball and basketball, she stuck with swimming as her main sport and added tennis for social interaction. She tried to play intramural basketball after school, but gave it up when a large girl on the opposing team arm-strangled Jenae as she dribbled toward the hoop, then put a fist in her face and said, "Give me the ball, bitch!" Jenae elbowed her back in the ribs and heard a whistle from the PE teacher/referee. "Foul on Jenae," she said. Jenae didn't argue, but she never returned and chose sports with lane lines and nets that separated contestants.

She became physically strong through sports and mentally tough through friendships, sibling relationships, and by doing hard things. Jenae's upbringing set her up to fly far from the nest . . . as her siblings did. She wanted to be authentic and loud and experience the world. She craved freedom.

———◆———

As a child, Neve was spoiled and undisciplined partly because he was too pretty. His mum's friends fawned over the perfect little boy with long eyelashes. Girls in primary school competed for his affection and he turned into the bullying, popular kid once puberty hit. His father hated it.

"Neve, you need to be more of a man. Maybe your attitude will change with a little hard work," Peter, his father, said.

"Aw dad, I don't want to be a construction worker like you. It's a filthy, hard life," teenaged Neve responded.

"What the fuck did you say, you little twit?" Peter's face turned red as he pulled Neve's ear and yelled in his face.

"I mean, look at you? Your face is always red because you spend half of your money getting pissed at the pub. Mum hates you, half of your kids hate you. Why would I want to be like you?"

Neve didn't back down. He'd grown to his father's height and looked him in the eyes as he pushed his father's shoulders away from him. Peter hit the ground on his bum, as his hands braced his fall. Other than a few grains of gravel stuck in his fleshy hands, Peter was unharmed. Neve miscalculated his father's strength and athleticism, and found himself in a half-Nelson restraint with no wiggle room.

"If you think you are such a tough bloke, prove it," Peter grunted and groaned.

"Get off of me, you washed up piece of shit. You think you are a big-time builder. 'I built this house, I built that hotel, I designed these duplexes.' I'm tired of hearing how great you are all of the time. Nothing I do is ever good enough for you," Neve said.

Peter released his grip on Neve and tossed him away like a rag doll.

"Things have got to change. I'll give you two options: Either commit to one year of boxing instruction to get some of your anger out; or go live with your auntie in Dunedin and help her on her sheep farm," Peter said, holding up his fingers. "You need to sweat hard and bleed a little to know what hard work really is," Peter added.

Neve's disdain for all things agricultural made the decision easy. He signed up for boxing lessons three days a week at a local gym. Neve struggled at first and often came home with red marks on his arms and face until he learned enough discipline to control his mind. In addition to repetitive practice hitting the speed bag and jumping rope, Neve was taught that boxing was 100% physical and 100% mental. He learned to train with intent by setting skill goals along the way. He made action plans to achieve bigger goals which perfected his craft to be a sharp, fast, and strong fighter.

On fight competition days, Peter attended Neve's events. Peter was proud to watch his son develop into a man physically and mentally, but couldn't stop himself from diminishing Neve's accomplishments.

"Hey dad, look at my second-place medal, it's heavy."

"What happened? Why didn't you win first place? Gold is better than silver. You were better than that guy." Peter walked away with a huff of disgust.

⸺◆⸺

Life became easier for everyone when Peter moved out of the family home and the divorce was final. Helen mustered enough courage to kick him out after their youngest daughter, Tee, started full-time boarding school. Helen found a decent paying job as an executive assistant and enjoyed working outside of the home. Peter's biggest complaint was that Helen started dating too soon after he was gone.

Neve earned high honors on his exit exams which qualified him for college. Helen was proud, but felt left behind when Neve chose to attend uni to study podiatry on the North Island. He picked podiatry because he wanted to help people but didn't want to commit to being a doctor for the whole body. *Feet should be easy enough,* Neve thought.

Dorm life was heaven for a young man who'd never been away from home. Stipends for food at the cafeteria were converted into beer bucks, and Neve often stayed out late partying on weeknights with his new friends. Neglecting to attend class was a hole he couldn't get out of, and he barely made it through the first semester with the bare minimum GPA. The writing was on the wall, but he wanted to stay because university was his first taste of real independence and he'd fallen in love with a girl for the first time.

Redemption was short lived and university life came to an abrupt end when Neve failed to bring his grades up and his first love broke his heart. He had no choice but to return to Christchurch with his tail tucked between his legs and a bouquet of flowers in his arms for his mum.

***

Neve humped his way by working odd jobs and applying for programs suggested by his friends.

"I think I found my calling. I got accepted to the police academy. I can see myself as a cop," Neve proclaimed to Helen.

"That might be a good fit for you Neve, yeah, I bet it will work out for you, with your experience in boxing and everything," Helen affirmed.

"Let's hope so. I'm out of options after this. I'll have to start over in another country if I screw this up."

Neve was genetically a physical specimen and his mental discipline still dwelled somewhere deep inside of him. But his restless pursuit for a bigger life would ultimately guide his future.

Chapter 4

Flying South

Logan

The first twelve hours riding in the back of a C-141 hidden in cargo nets behind large armaments was painful, but Logan was grateful that he was going to make it safely to the Philippines in a few more hours. The plane had been refueled twice in flight by KC-135 Stratotankers – once, as they passed by the Hawaiian Islands and finally after passing Guam. Half way through the flight, Bart slipped away after using the head and brought Logan an extra bagged lunch and a water bottle. Bart made his way back to the flight deck to retrieve a blanket and a small pillow when he saw Logan shivering in the cargo hold. Bart tossed them like a football and Logan snatched them in mid-air.

"If you have to piss, use the plastic bottle," Bart said.

"Thanks dude. I'll never forget what you did," Logan said.

"You better forget it and never bring it up. I'll deny it if you say a word to anyone."

"Like I said, I won't hurt anyone again. I just want a new life . . . a second chance."

The only people who knew Logan was still alive was Captain Bart and four Filipino women he'd been writing to over the past few months.

Before staging his own suicide, Logan withdrew large sums of money from his bank accounts and stockpiled over $20,000, which he carried in his duffle bag along with a few other necessities. Gummy bears kept his mouth moist and his brain temporarily fueled, but Bart's peanut butter sandwich from the sack lunch was a welcome punch of protein.

Logan had killed four and a half months in Joshua Tree National Park figuring out a way to escape the country undetected. In between crafting blackmail letters to former colleagues, he scoured mail-order-bride magazines and reread tattered pornographic materials. He had access to a beat-up RV parked in the harsh sand-scape that he had used to hide human assets for weeks at a time when he was still a respected FBI agent. When he drove to his postal box in a dusty town outside of the park, he wondered why his life had been cursed and prickly – like the thick, thorned, cacti that surrounded him. Perhaps a new environment could help him become kind and desirable.

Girls from the Philippines were eager to connect with him, especially because he sent them each ten dollars with every letter so that they could afford to write him back. Most return letters contained drawings of suggestive images because the ladies he'd connected with needed an interpreter to communicate in English.

But one special girl, Joy Lyn, could read and write English. Joy Lyn was different from the other girls; she was educated, obedient to her father, and went to church every Sunday with her close-knit family.

Her family lived near a large American Naval and Air Force base where she worked as domestic help for a newly wedded American couple. Officers were expected to hire Filipinos to help enhance the local economy. She cleaned and cooked local dishes for families while her dad, Pepe, took on landscaping duties for the neighborhood block. Joy Lyn grew fond of American men.

A Catholic upbringing formed her values which included saving herself for marriage. Nearby, at a gated large property run by nuns, Joy Lyn volunteered on Saturdays for a large orphanage. She was reminded every week that sex had consequences. Mixed-race babies were the largest population and presumed to have American GI fathers.

Due to poverty and unrest, many Filipino fathers wanted their daughters to marry an American, move to San Diego, and get a Honda and a house so that the rest of the family could follow. Joy Lyn only wanted to find a man who would stay with her in the Philippines so that she could remain close to her mother and father. Although her country was in upheaval after the exile of Ferdinand Marcos, and had rumblings of a coup against Corazon Aquino, she was attached to the wildness and kindness it had to offer.

———◆◇◆———

Logan dreamed about seeing Joy Lyn face to face for the first time. He hoped that their chemistry would spark immediately when their eyes locked, and they would be happy together for the rest of their lives. Recurring thoughts of Joy Lyn kept his mind occupied, making the frigid fifteen-hour flight more tolerable.

Captain Bart squinted his eyes and turned his head to the side with his chin raised as he strained to understand the Manila Center air traffic control over the radio. The frequency was staticky and controllers' accents were thick. Exhaustion had set in even though two relief pilots filled in over the Pacific Ocean. Two flight engineers and one load master took over responsibility for the aircraft once they landed and tires were chocked into place.

Logan stretched and blew warm breath into the palms of his hands to get circulation in his body moving. He knew he had a small window of time to escape without being noticed, and took his chance once the flight crew deplaned and before the ground personnel showed up to unload cargo. His legs tingled and felt numb as he lowered himself down the metal ladder and dropped to a warm tarmac below. Cover of early morning darkness allowed him to duck and run behind the nearest hangar. And the smell of pre-dawn humid air felt like a beautiful bouquet of welcome even though nobody was there for him.

Bart leaned against a hangar door through a thick window with small wires running diagonally through it, and watched Logan maneuver off base. The guilt he felt for aiding and abetting such an asshole was mitigated by rationalizing that Logan had been removed from the country he loved. Bart loved his family more, and they were worth the risk of bringing Logan to the Philippines illegally. He knew Logan was capable of unspeakable acts, but gave him a 50/50 chance of making his life right by starting over with a clean slate.

Logan's plan was to find his own way to the small town where Joy Lyn lived. She wasn't expecting him, but he was certain she'd be pleasantly surprised. With a black duffle bag on his shoulder to conceal his face, Logan made his way off base, onto the main road and waited at a bus stop.

Chapter 5

Second Thoughts

Jenae - Logan

She had a raging urge to feel herself wrapped in Neve's arms again. But Jenae's mother didn't understand her need to move so far away from her – New Zealand was by far the greatest distance away from wheat fields in the heartland. Her siblings were far flung around the world and it was Jenae's first opportunity to beat them at the living abroad game.

Her twin brothers set their lives up in Tokyo after spending a year studying abroad there. Sister had ventured to Bordeaux, France for her junior year in college; specifically chosen for the wine region. Niles worked offshore oil rigs in the Middle East and feared for his life when he and his girlfriend were arrested in Dubai for displaying a passionate kiss in front of a hotel. Eldest brother took clandestine visits to parts of the world that were probably further than New Zealand, but were never discussed openly, therefore deemed irrelevant in Jenae's made-up competition.

"What are you going to do when you get homesick and want to move back to the States?" Mom argued.

"I haven't thought that far ahead yet, Mom."

"Exactly! You could find yourself in dangerous situations and your father and I couldn't be there for you."

Jenae had kept a lot of stories from her parents including stalking incidents by Logan. She didn't want to worry them and knew she could handle the situation.

"There's more to the story, Mom."

"Are you pregnant? Oh my, if you are pregnant, then you need to stay near your father and me. I could help raise my grandchild," Mom beamed with hope.

"Mom, NO. I'm not pregnant."

Jenae filled her in on the stalking incidents that started in Hawaii and continued in Dallas and San Francisco.

"I thought he was dead, until I found a note from him at my graduation ceremony. It was really creepy. . . like him."

"Oh, honey. I get it. I know you think you can handle it by yourself, but shouldn't you call the police? They could protect you from him, instead of moving halfway across the planet!"

"I don't think that would do any good. Besides, Neve makes me feel safe and I see my future with him. He promised that he wants to return to the States one day, so we can be on the same continent again. I'll be back."

"Why don't you just wait until he finishes his flight training and gets his visa worked out? Why do you have to leave me?"

"Mom, we live halfway across the country away from each other now."

"I know, but it feels different. You'd be half a world away. Why do my children leave me behind? Who's going to take care of me when I'm old and infirm? I always thought it would be you."

"Your dramatics are impressive. Just plan a trip with Dad to visit me in New Zealand this year. I'm sure we won't live there forever and you can brag to your church friends that you visited your handsome son-in-law down under."

"My what? Did you get married without telling us?"

"No, no, no. But we might get married over there so that I can stay and work. It will be a simple ceremony. I promise we can have a beautiful wedding in the U.S. when we get back."

Jenae's mom feigned distress, but was secretly pleased and relieved that her twenty-seven-year-old daughter had finally found a husband.

The thought of moving so far away was daunting and Jenae thought her mother had raised some good points. New Zealand was more than a day's flight away from her parents. She had very little money and Neve was spending all of his savings on flight lessons. What if he failed his exams and it was all for naught? They would have to start over again. What if Neve decided that he never wanted to leave his family again. Helen was a formidable force and she fawned over her favorite son.

Jenae ruminated over her decision to leave or stay; if she didn't take the leap, the love of her life that took a lifetime to find would slip through her hands. Could she find another partner who loved to travel, who thought is was funny every time she beat him in Scrabble, or tried to steal kisses in the most inappropriate places? How many men would rub her feet as they sat on the couch and watched rugby and football and discussed world problems. They were opposites in a lot of ways, which seemed to made them compatible.

⚬

Logan missed the only bus of the day headed in the direction of Joy Lyn's town. A short statured Negrito waiting on the bench next to him smiled, nodded and pointed to the map posted on a stand. Bleary-eyed and exhausted, Logan followed him onto a bus headed for Manila. His big feet stomped his way down a grimy floor, while he held onto seat tops and swayed like a boat captain. He plopped into the last window seat at the back of the bus.

A heavy hot breeze hit his face creating beads of sweat above his eyebrows as he gazed past the sun low in the sky. He had just survived a freezing cargo hold and was grateful that his bones had started to thaw. Logan took in the sights and got more excited as he saw signs advertising the entertainment district. As the bus flew down a mostly dirt road, overgrown vegetation scraped an open window nearly grazing Logan's face as he leaned out to read billboards on the side of the road. Most advertised bars and brothels all rolled into one, and Logan's favorite was the *Eager Beaver.* He thought it had a catchy name, beers were only 25 cents, and all of their girls had current VD cards.

Logan's rebirth could wait another week while he got his bearings and made a plan to win Joy Lyn as his wife.

The best hotel Logan could find in the entertainment district sold rooms by the hour, but the manager gave him a regular room rate for a special suite on the shady side of the building. Logan paid for a week, and felt like a king when he looked in his duffle bag and smiled at a stack of bills that would last him at least a year in the Philippines.

A huge American military presence in the country wasn't appreciated by many Filipinos, but Logan was prepared and had worked on a new identity while hiding out in the desert. He'd perfected his Australian accent to reinvent himself to become more accepted by the locals.

His favorite phrase was "chock a block," meaning crowded. That's how most of Manila felt to him, especially on public transportation. A converted Jeepney with a dozen people clinging to hang on, zoomed by the hotel with an engine roar.

"How many people do those Jeepney's hold? They all look chock a block," Logan asked the innkeeper.

"The answer to that is . . . always one more," he said with a grin as he counted out U.S dollar bills.

Once Logan escaped U.S. soil, he had the freedom to let loose and be himself. Instead of being the watcher with an FBI badge, the past few months he found himself constantly looking over his own shoulder. The mental and emotional stress was exhausting.

A long sleep under a fan during the heat of the day rejuvenated and reinvigorated Logan 2.0. A cool shower and shave made him feel like a million bucks, and new sandals and clothes from the market made him look the part. He had the *Eager Beaver* in his sights, but stopped in at a restaurant that advertised lots of fried meat dishes. Logan wasn't a fan of vegetables, but could handle them wrapped up in Lumpia rolls, especially with sweet dipping sauce. He also choked down some Balut with a San Miguel beer. He'd heard that eating fermented local foods would make him smell like a local which would help conceal his American identity. Logan smiled deviously as he wondered if Jenae was allergic to duck eggs in addition to chicken eggs. As he ate a pork dish, Lechon, his eyes gazed at the ceiling and his mind wandered back to what Jenae was doing. *Hm, I wonder if she freaked out from my graduation card. She looked so carefree at her ceremony. I just wanted her to know that I was thinking about her. I wonder if she's still with that Kiwi. God, I hated that guy. He was so pretentious. Acting like I didn't love her first. I have his address in my contacts, maybe I'll have to pay him a visit if I ever get*

over to New Zealand. I wonder if Jenae has gotten any of my
other letters.

Chapter 6

Union

Jenae - Neve

A Kiwi accent over the intercom was barely audible over constant whooshing of air at 435 knots. He said something about tray tables and seat-backs. She had already filled out her second customs entry form. The first, she accidentally doodled hearts and practiced writing her soon to be new married name on it. On one last visit to the lavatory to freshen up, Jenae's blood shot eyes stung when she inserted contact lenses onto her eyeballs. Cool saline solution eventually felt refreshing after a long uncomfortable sleep on the 14-hour flight to Auckland.

Her third trip to New Zealand was different from her first two visits in the past year. It felt more permanent and exciting. Neve was meeting her at the gate in Auckland when she landed. He had flown in from Christchurch and had a big weekend planned for the two of them before their return flight to the South Island.

Jenae gathered three large bags off of the revolving apparatus and loaded them on a free cart left behind by another passenger. The customs line was lengthy by the time she visited the loo and changed into a brand-new outfit.

A red-headed lady tugged on the back of her shirt.

"Do you want me to pop this tag off for you, Miss?"

"Oh, thank you! Yes please."

"That's a beautiful white blouse, so fancy!"

"Thanks, I want to look nice for my fiancé. He's meeting me here. I think he has something special planned."

"I'm sure he will be pleased to see you, dear."

An early bird flight to Auckland was a challenge for Neve to get to after his blokes took him out for a last-minute bachelor party. They'd figured out that Neve had planned a wedding weekend for him and Jenae on the North Island and couldn't let him get away without a night out at a strip club on Hereford Street. As the groom, dancers gave Neve extra attention. They rubbed their cleavage in his face and bent over in black G-strings and lace topped thigh-high hose held up with garter belts. Attempts by the ladies to extract every dollar from his blokes was successful and although he was aroused, Neve and his friends ran out of money before the private backroom action. The thought of explaining it away to Jenae was far too dangerous.

Neve's eyes were closed for exactly forty minutes before his alarm beeped and beeped again. A quick shower never got quite warm enough, but woke him up with goosebumps. On his way out the door, he left a note for his mum.

"Left early to catch a plane. Picking up Jenae in Auckland. Will be back in a few days, XO Neve."

Luckily, he had packed the day before, and yellow gold wedding bands were secured in a pocket of his black suitcase. Brand new charcoal dress pants and a crisp white shirt were neatly folded with tissue paper from the men's department at the fanciest department store on Victoria Street.

A commuter plane sat at Gate Four in the dark as Neve handed his ticket to the agent standing at the door. As the last passenger to board, the flight attendant pointed to a spot left in an overhead bin to place his suitcase. He stepped quietly and whispered because he didn't want to disturb the seemingly sleeping passengers buckled in their seats waiting for take-off.

A nap made the time fly by and just before landing he gulped down a cup of strong, cool Earl Gray tea that had been served to him shortly after leaving Christchurch. As he leaned into the aisle and looked toward the closed cockpit door, the flight attendant tapped him on the shoulder from behind.

"Aren't you Tee's brother? I went to school with her. My sister was in your class, I think."

"Yep, yeah, yeah. I'm Neve. Give your sister my best." Neve said in a pitched voice two levels higher than normal. He didn't recognize the girl, possibly because he was hungover and groggy. After he had a few minutes of shuteye and thoughts of a great night out with his blokes, Neve got the scaries. His eyes widened and he moaned as he tried to slow his breathing. He felt his heart beating at a fast clip in his chest and nausea set in. It was a temporary moment of panic over what he had planned that weekend. He was getting married.

———◆———

Neve waited outside customs with a bouquet of aromatic freesias, and cranked his neck every time a shadowy figure moved down the narrow, tiled hallway behind electronic doors. Nausea had subsided, but his hands still quaked as he looked around the airport. A young family waited with a hand painted sign, "Hoki mai ra." Neve didn't retain much Maori language that he learned in primary school, but he did recognize, "Welcome home."

He patted down the outside pocket of his suitcase, and pulled out the marriage license that he had gotten earlier that week. They had a 2 PM appointment at the courthouse to get married.

After Neve finished whiffing his armpits to make sure he cleaned all of his stench off in the washroom, he looked up and locked eyes with Jenae. Her smile lit up the dark passageway as she squealed with delight. *Swish, squawk,* the doors magically opened and she passed through and flew into Neve's arms.

All of Neve's nerves washed away with the tears he shed while holding on to her for dear life.

Impossibilities were soon to be their future together.

———— ◆◇◆ ————

A Gothic Revival courthouse in the center of Auckland was more than Jenae could have hoped for. She imagined their courthouse marriage would be in a cold office section of a 1970's modern monstrosity. Instead, the red brick building with towers and gargoyles housed a wood beamed high ceiling courtroom with ornate carvings. A judge's bench resembled an altar at a church, which created a hallowed ceremony.

The bouquet of flowers that Neve bought for her popped against Jenae's frilly, cream-colored, modest blouse and A-line satin skirt. Jenae pulled a flower from the bundle and placed it in the lapel of Neve's charcoal suit.

When the clock tower struck twice, the officiant appeared from behind a royal red velvet curtain and the ceremony began.

I am authorized by the Government of Aotearoa New Zealand to conduct this ceremony as a registered marriage celebrant. Neville and Jenae, in marrying, you are making a sincere commitment to go forward in your lives formally united as partners – promising support and encouragement to each other throughout your lives together.

However, no ceremony can create a marriage; only the two of you can do that by supporting, trusting, and respecting each other, in all that you share together.

Neville and Jenae. We come now to your marriage vows, which are the legally binding words that confirm your choice to marry and declare your commitment to each other.

New Zealand law requires that each of you declares before me, and at least two other witnesses, that you are freely entering into this marriage and that you take the other person to be your legally wedded wife or husband.

I will ask each of you now to repeat this statement after me.

Neville . . . I, Neville, am freely entering into this marriage and take you, Jenae, to be my legal wife.

"I, Neville, am freely entering into this marriage and take you, Jenae, to be my legal wife," Neve repeated.

Now Jenae . . . I, Jenae, am freely entering into this marriage and take you, Neville, to be my legal husband.

"I, Jenae, am freely entering into this marriage and take you, Neve or Neville, to be my legal husband," Jenae repeated with a nervous giggle.

Today you have chosen to exchange rings. A wedding ring is a symbol of the marriage vows you have just made. May these rings always remind you of your commitment to each other.

I now invite you to exchange rings.

Neve reached out for Jenae's left hand and kissed it before sliding a gold wedding band next to her diamond engagement ring. Jenae held her hand up and stared at the shining symbol of her future. She realigned her rings and reached for Neve's hand. Instead of kissing his hand, she wiped beads of sweat from his forehead and a tiny tear from his eye. She slipped his wedding band on with a sigh of relief and tucked the crumpled tissue behind her bouquet.

Neville and Jenae, it is my great pleasure to pronounce you legally married – Husband and Wife. Neville, you may now kiss your bride.

Congratulations. Tena rawa atu korua!

Two official witnesses provided by the court for a reasonable fee walked forward to the officiant. They signed the newlywed's paperwork and the man handed the documents to Neve, and said, "Good on ya." The woman smiled at Jenae. "You are a beautiful bride. I pray your days ahead are filled with love – just like today."

The celebrant imparted his final words, "This document is confirmation of your marriage – Go well."

The female witness doubled as a photographer and kindly clicked pictures of the newlyweds on Neve's 35 mm camera. Jenae directed her own photo session that started with reenacting the first marital kiss, and ended on the front steps of the courthouse with birds chirping their approval in the fir trees nearby.

Even though they married in a courthouse, Neve vowed to be faithful to Jenae in front of God with humility and certainty.

Chapter 7

Honeymoon
Neve and Jenae

Clouds closed in on the otherwise perfect May-day and skies released a heavy mist. The newlyweds barely noticed except to dance in the rain as they scurried to a taxi waiting for them on the street.

"Where to, young lovers?" The cabbie asked.

"Take us to the ferry building downtown please. We have a boat to catch," Neve instructed while he held Jenae's hand.

"Where are we going, Neve? Are you saving our honeymoon as a surprise?" Jenae said.

Without much money left in his bank account, a ferry ride to a nearby island was all he could afford. The wedding weekend he'd planned off of the North Island was exotic for both him and Jenae. Neve rarely traveled across the Cook Straight, except to catch an international flight out of Auckland.

The couple wrangled all of Jenae's bags and made their way to the dock. A luxurious yacht was parked a few slips over, and although Jenae had high hopes, she knew that a weekend on a yacht was something to look forward to in a few decades, but not now. When Neve returned with tickets for the next ferry, a worker followed and tagged and tossed her bags onto a cart that would be stowed in the bottom of the boat for the forty-minute ride.

"So, where are we going? How long will we be gone?" Jenae looked up at Neve's soft lips as she wrapped both arms around his waist. He leaned in and kissed her lips and then her forehead.

"See that island over there, just past the clouds?" Neve pointed across the bay.

"Yeah, I can kind of make it out."

"That's Waiheke Island. It is still part of Auckland and well known for its wineries. I've made hotel reservations for us at one of the more famous vineyards. We can do activities if the weather holds up, or we can stay in our suite and rest up." Neve winked.

"The name sounds a lot like Waikiki, like where we met," Jenae smiled.

"Maybe I picked it subconsciously, but I hear it's a romantic place."

"So, you've never been there before?" Jenae asked with a tinge of suspicious jealousy.

"Nope, you are my first and last travel partner. You are all I need, Jenae." Neve put his arm around her shoulders and kissed her on the cheek.

Skies cleared and sunlight glowed as the ferry navigated outside sail boats moored in the island's bay beyond the tide's reach. Neve and Jenae stood on the front bow arm in arm as wind whisked around their melded bodies until the ferryboat safely docked. The sea behind them glimmered as the sun set in an autumn orange and blue hue.

With luggage safely contained in the boot of a rental car in the dirt parking lot adjacent to the dock, Neve and Jenae kissed and petted in the front seat until the sun finally sunk into the ocean. Neither had made such a commitment before, but both carried no doubt that they had made the correct decision.

The honeymoon suite had privacy and a view of rolling hills with vineyards and a bay below. A standing claw foot tub on the patio and wood burning fireplace in the living area had to wait. Exhaustion had set in and the couple fell asleep in each other's arms, still dressed in their wedding attire.

⊰•◦O◦•⊱

Tiptoeing around a small kitchen in the suite, Jenae opened a small refrigerator stocked with breakfast foods. Bacon, eggs, fruit, yogurt, orange juice, milk, and a package of *Vogels* toast was a welcome find for a girl whose last meal was served 30,000 feet over the Pacific Ocean. Neve remained unconscious, face down in a fluffy pillow while she fried up the bacon on low and prepared hot water for tea and instant coffee.

Jenae had returned from a walk around the vineyard to take in the sunrise over the bay. Cool bright blue skies awoke feelings of awe and amazement. She struck up a conversation with another couple who were courteous enough for New Zealanders, and told her about their favorite activities around the island, and clued her into breakfast supplies in the kitchen.

"Rise and shine, hubby!" Jenae set a tray with yogurt, fruit and a cup of hot tea on the bedside table next to his head. She ran her fingers through his short, brown, thick hair, and scratched his back as he made waking moans.

"Good morning, wifey." Neve rolled over, grabbed her around the waist, and pulled Jenae on top of him. She giggled and kissed his face all over in a series of pecks, ending in a long deep French kiss that made her body tingle and her back arch. Jenae unbuttoned Neve's dress shirt from their wedding and unbuckled his belt. Jenae easily slipped out of her track suit and they consummated their marriage as quickly as the bacon cooked to a crisp.

"Mm, bacon and orgasms. Two of my favorite things," Neve said.

"It doesn't take much to make you happy. I can't believe we're married!" She said as she lifted her left hand with her wedding band on display with her cheeks aglow.

A boat with yellow sails in Oneroa Bay floated in clear blue waters within a stone's throw from shore. The newlyweds sat at an outdoor cafe in a village by the sea and ate beet and buffalo cheese dip with crostinis and a local brew for lunch. Jenae stuck with a light pilsner beer and Neve tried a fruity IPA. A young couple walked past pushing a pram with the bonnet extended.

"We should find some sunscreen at a shop before we go for a sail. There's a hole in the ozone down here. It's easy to get sunburned . . . especially at this time of year," Neve explained.

"A hole?" Jenae asked.

"Yeah, it was created from CFCs in aerosols . . . you know. Ozone protects people and plants from UV rays."

"I'm lost. Is this a thing?" Jenae asked.

"From what I remember in my chemistry class, oxygen gas, and free oxygen atoms are constantly being combined, broken apart, and recombined in the stratosphere. Reactions are driven by the energy from UV radiation, which is absorbed in the process." Neve carefully gestured and moved his hands to make his point.

"What? Is that real? I thought it was just a doomsday threat."

"No, we really do have a hole in the atmosphere down here that moves around near the South Pole. They say the breakdown is from spray deodorant and hairspray."

"That sounds silly and should be easy to fix – just ban aerosols. Although, I do like aerosol deodorants better than stick," Jenae said.

"There's a ban in the works; hopefully the hole will close up when aerosols go away," Neve said.

◄О►

While applying sunscreen on their noses, the newlyweds sat on a wooden dock while the sailboat owner navigated closer. Neve wasn't keen on boats, but Jenae acted extra excited about an advert in a brochure that was left in their honeymoon suite. He remembered how much fun they'd had together on their first date on a catamaran ride off of Waikiki beach. Tension eased as the calming effect of alcohol from beer at lunch kicked in.

"Alrighty then mates. I'm your captain for our three-hour sail. Hopefully the winds will pick up a little bit so that we can get a wake going, but if not, we'll have a great time relaxing," a ruddy-faced sailor with mussed blonde hair said as he helped the couple onto the small boat.

"A three-hour tour, huh. Is your first mate's name Gilligan by chance?" Jenae grabbed his hand and leaned on the captain as she stepped gingerly onto the craft.

"Ah, I see you have life jackets, just in case we get into rough waters." Jenae pointed to Neve as he looked around pensively.

"Yeah, yeah. The jackets are there if we need them, there's plenty for everyone. But we are staying close to shore, so no worries. No weather has shown up in the forecast, and it should be smooth sailing. We're waiting on one other couple and then we will shove off soon," the captain motioned.

"What's the occasion for your visit to our paradise island?"

"We just got married! This is our wedding weekend holiday," Jenae replied.

"Until we can afford a proper honeymoon," Neve defended under his breath.

"Ah, I suspected as much. I could see the sparkle of new love in your eyes. As promised, I packed a couple local bottles of wine and some snacks for our stop at Cactus Bay. It's considered by a lot of Waihekans as the most perfect beach. Along with Garden Cove, it's very romantic. I think you'll like it. It's only accessible by a boat like mine, or by kayak. We'll give you some time to take it all in."

"That sounds lovely!" Jenae responded in a sing-song voice.

After final passengers boarded, the helper pushed the boat from the dock and jumped on as it drifted away. Newly embarked love birds were sufficiently sauced up on local wine and stayed to themselves. They pecked at each-other's faces with coos and kisses at the front of the boat for the entire journey to Cactus Beach.

Sails were raised and the boat turned to catch advantageous winds that propelled them along the coastline. Cool breezes blew Jenae's hair flat against her head while Neve held her from behind in an attempt to keep her warm.

The beach landing got sporty when errant waves pushed and pulled the boat as passengers disembarked by jumping on the sand with a hand held by the boat captain.

"Yikes, the water is cold." Jenae's rolled up pants got splashed as she hopped onto dry land.

"You can explore the cove while I set up some refreshments for the four of you," the captain directed after all of the passengers were safely on shore.

"Let's hike up this hill and see what's up there," Neve suggested as he grabbed Jenae's hand. They scrambled up a beaten down grass path with spiky plants and bushes dotted across the hillside. Jenae huffed and puffed to the top of the vista.

"OK, this is good enough for me. I want to take in the beauty for a moment." She put her hands on her hips and sucked in fresh air through her nostrils to slow her breathing.

"Hey, here are some flat boulders we can sit on. Look, there's a Cessna 172 directly in front of us." Neve pointed into the sun.

A small plane flew straight over them and they waved at the pilot as he banked toward the bay.

"Cool! It looked like there were passengers in there. I want to take a plane ride for our next activity," Neve said with more enthusiasm than he'd expressed about the boat ride.

"That's fine with me. But don't you get tired of flying?"

"I love it and I need all the experience I can get." Neve hadn't mustered up the nerve to tell Jenae about needing to retest for his license because he failed the first time around. It cost him a lot of money and time and he didn't want to ruin the mood on their wedding weekend.

A picnic blanket with a basket was set up on the beach by the first mate, who waved his arms and pointed to get their attention. A bottle of local Chardonnay was opened next to two glasses with a plate of cheese, crackers and red grapes. They toasted to a life together, kissed and drank. Neve had grown to like Chardonnay when he lived in San Francisco. It was his next favorite beverage behind a perfectly poured draft beer with a foam head. Jenae picked individual grapes off of the bunch and alternated feeding them to Neve and to herself.

"One for you, one for me. Two for you, one two for me," She giggled more loudly as the wine tickled her brain.

They leaned back on their forearms and watched the other couple from the boat playfully push each other on a rope swing strung up on a tree at the edge of the beach. The woman leaned back and hung on to the rope with straight stretched out arms. Her long straight hair hung down behind with her ankles crossed in front while her lover tried to grab her bottom each time she returned.

—◆O◆—

While waiting to re-board the sailboat, the couples struck up a conversation to fill awkward silence.

"How long are you visiting the island?" Jenae asked.

"Ah, just one more night. We stopped over on our holiday from Australia. And you?"

"Yeah, we've got two more nights – three in all. We just got married in downtown Auckland," Neve responded.

"Brilliant! Congratulations. I hear an accent. Are you Canadian?" he asked Jenae.

"Close, but no. I'm from California in America. I guess I live here now," Jenae said bashfully.

"Right. Well, you should visit Australia while you're in this hemisphere. We have furry animals and snakes," the woman added.

"I've never been, but I have friends in Adelaide. So it's highly likely we'll get over there soon," Jenae said.

Neve and Jenae lounged in each other's arms at the helm of the boat on the sail back to Oneroa Bay. A magical sunset led the way.

— ◆ —

A local musician serenaded diners at the fanciest restaurant on the island. Candlelight flickered in hurricane lanterns surrounding the dining room and a single candle burned bright next to a flower vase with her favorite freesias on their table for two. Jenae usually didn't eat raw seafood, but she ordered fresh oysters out of the bay and scallops lightly sautéed in garlic butter. She prayed that the half bottle of wine with her meal would kill bacteria and prevent food poisoning.

"I'm disappointed they don't have mussels on the menu. I guess El Niño has affected our supply this year," Neve said as he carved up a sirloin steak soaked in a butter glaze.

"I'm surprised you didn't go for rack of lamb. I know it's a specialty of New Zealand," Jenae said.

"It's really big on the South Island. You'll see when you spend more time there. But I'm not really a fan of the taste. I'll have it at big holiday dinners, but steak is my favorite." Neve dipped a chunk of steak in a dollop of purple mashed potatoes.

⸺◈⸺

Timing was perfect for the only available sightseeing flight the next day. Noontime was late enough to sleep in with a romp in the sheets and early enough that Jenae didn't need to eat. Her stomach churned with the ups and downs of a small aircraft, especially after a night of wine tasting. Waxed sick-sacks stuck in the side panel of the Cessna's backseat caught her eye and she pulled one out and opened it, just in case.

From the back bench, she saw Neve pointing to a dial in front of him and then to switches on the ceiling of the cockpit. His mouth was moving while the pilot smiled and nodded, but Jenae could only hear muffled sounds over revving engines. In a lurch, the plane turned to white lines on the runway and quickly sped into the air, lifting the three wheels and three passengers off of the pavement. Neve looked back, gave her a smile and grabbed her knee. He mouthed, "Are you OK?" She put the sick-sack between her knees and gave him a thumbs up. Neve pointed to head phones tucked in a pocket of the back of the pilot's seat, and motioned for her to put them on.

He adjusted the microphone arm attached to his head phones and said, "Are you OK, love?" Jenae smiled and nodded. The pilot followed up with, "Just tap me on the shoulder if you need anything."

"AOK," she said awkwardly. Focusing on the voice of the pilot distracted her from dizziness in her head.

"We're over the Hauraki Gulf and you can see most of the twenty-five miles of beach on Waiheke. This is known as the island of wine and we have approximately 6,000 residents on the island – just ten percent are Maori. Much of the eastern islands are the remains of a Miocene volcano, which erupted 15 million years ago," the pilot announced over the headphones.

"Look down there. We were on Cactus Bay yesterday," Jenae pointed down and smudged her window with her pointing finger.

"And that's where we started our boat ride at Oneroa Beach," Neve added.

"Behind us is Stony Batter. Three World War Two emplacements are on the eastern edge over there," the pilot directed. "And ahead of us are two clothing-optional beaches called Little Palm and Onetangi. Warning . . . most of the sunbathers should be wearing full tracksuits to spare the rest of us from nightmares about lumpy, naked people."

The flight made a pass over Ponui, Pakihi and Rangitoto islands before turning back to the airstrip. Although the airplane ride wasn't the least bit romantic, Jenae lovingly watched Neve take in the experience because she knew it made him happy. Jenae had a lot to learn about her new husband in his country that she now called home. She did know that she felt his love and protection and could see them together for the rest of their lives.

Chapter 8

Reality Bites

Jenae and Neve

Helen was absent from the house when Neve and Jenae returned from Christchurch airport, but she left fresh meat pies for them on the kitchen counter with a note. "Welcome home! Sorry I had to work. Be home for dinner – XO." Neve smelled them before placing them on a paper towel in the microwave and pouring two glasses of orange juice.

Jenae was grateful to have a place to stay, but picked up the newspaper sitting on a loveseat to check out "apartment rental" ads in the back section. Her chest got tight and had trouble taking deep breaths when she thought about sharing a living space with anyone other than her new husband.

"Look, here's a place right on North Hagley Park. It's a high rise on Carlton Mill Road." Jenae circled the small printed ad with a pencil, folded the paper into fourths and handed it to Neve. "I bet it has fantastic views and the location is central to everywhere."

"You'll need to find a job quickly to afford that right now. Remember, I'm juggling part-time work with house flipping and investing, plus I'm paying for flying lessons. The only way I've stayed afloat is because my mum charges me a nominal rent right now," Neve warned as he handed the paper back to Jenae.

"She charges you rent? Huh. I've got money saved from my insurance settlement from when that guy totaled my car while I was at work. Plus, I didn't need to spend my last two paychecks on anything. I think we'll be fine. Can we at least look at it?"

"I don't know, Jenae. It's on a high floor, well not the penthouse, but I'm sure it's still out of our price range."

"Well, I'm going to look for a job now because I want that apartment! Don't underestimate your wife." Jenae leaned back on a loveseat and turned newspaper pages to "help wanted."

"Good luck! The economy isn't the best around here. Maybe you can find a healthcare job doing something." Neve was proud of her tenacity and a little bit turned on by her confidence.

"Ye of little faith." Jenae circled three jobs on one page before Neve washed and dried their dishes in the sink.

"I don't think I can get a nursing job, I'm not licensed here yet. Besides, I don't really want one. That's why I got my MBA." Jenae moved the paper closer to her face to read the tiny print. "Here's one for a pharmaceutical sales representative. It asks for healthcare and business experience. I'm perfect for it."

"How old is that paper? The job may be filled already."

"Oh crap, it's from last week, but they're accepting applications postmarked by . . . tomorrow."

"You aren't going to make it, Jenae. They expect a professional photo and a CV. You just got here. You haven't even unpacked."

Jenae raised her index finger, smiled and jogged upstairs to their bedroom. She opened a big suitcase and found her 35 mm camera with five unused pictures on the film roll. From a different bag laid out on the carpet, she pulled out her newly purchased navy-blue Tahari suit jacket and a file of paperwork then laid them out on the bed.

"Can you take some pictures of me after I get ready?" Jenae hollered from the top of the stairs to Neve who was sorting through bills at the kitchen table.

"Sure. But you better hurry up if you want good lighting."

<hr>

The shower took forever to warm up, but it gave Jenae time to pull out her make-up bag, electrical adapter and plug in her curling iron. She reached up and wiggled her fingers in tepid warm water drizzling from the shower head and hung a bath towel on the door handle that she grabbed from the hallway closet.

Jenae prided herself on efficiency. She could get herself showered and coiffed in under fifteen minutes – twenty with curled hair.

"I'm ready for my photo shoot! Just make sure you take pictures from the waist up." Jenae popped out of the stairway in full make up and smoothed wavy hair wearing a suit jacket on top and panties on her bottom.

"Sexy! You'll certainly get the job in that outfit." Neve kidded.

"I didn't have time to worry about my skirt. Besides, it's kind of wrinkled. I only have five shots, so don't screw around. Keep the camera up here." She pointed to her chin as she sat in a chair set up next to sliding glass doors.

"Say cheese – one, two, three." Neve directed.

"Cheese!"

"OK, now turn your head left and look back toward me. Say cheese."

"Cheese!"

"Now the other side."

"OK, but I want two serious looks to finish."

"Got it. I hope they come out. Let's run to the mall to get them developed at the one-hour counter. We should make it before they close and then we can pick up some groceries for dinner." Neve waited as Jenae ran upstairs to change back into her tracksuit.

"Does Helen have a typewriter, or do I need to go to a library tomorrow?" Jenae asked as she buckled into the left passenger seat.

"Yeah, yeah. She was a secretary. I think she has stationery paper too."

"I can work on my cover letter and rework my resume tomorrow. I'm going to get this job. I can feel it, and we are going to move into that apartment!"

———◆———

As much as Helen wanted her own home back to herself again, she understood Neve's insecurity of having failed his initial flight test. He needed to pass to continue his dream career. She had lent him funds from her retirement account to cover some of his flight time and instruction. They were both invested in his success.

"I'm so happy that you're here, and you are part of our family now – my first daughter-in-law. I wish the family could have been there for the wedding." Helen gave Jenae a passing hug from above as she took a seat at the kitchen table.

"Sorry, Mum. It was beautiful in the court house, but we plan on having a formal wedding reception with a dress and flowers and festivities sometime in the near future. Jenae's parents might come out at Christmas time. Maybe we can have a fancy party then," Neve reassured.

"I better make friends quickly to invite!" Jenae said.

"You'll meet people easier if you have a job." Helen filled her glass with the remaining drops of wine from a bottle brought from Waiheke Island.

"Don't worry, I'm already working on a few job listings. In fact, can I borrow your typewriter to update my CV to send out tomorrow? We found an apartment available near Hagley Park, too."

Jenae's fast paced approach paid off. The pharmaceutical company received her resume and professional photos before the deadline – via same day Fast Post mail. Flynn, a sales manager for the South Island, called Jenae two days later to invite her for an interview at a hotel suite near the airport. He apologized about the short notice, "Tomorrow is our final day for interviews for two positions on the South Island and we want to give you a chance. My fiancée and I just got back from a two-month road trip from America. I loved it.!"

A Tahari blue suit from Nordstrom with silk hose and pumps may have been overkill for their interview. Jenae looked like the boss, but her friendly demeanor and willingness to listen to the highlights of Flynn's holiday gave an air of authenticity. The last interview of the day lasted beyond the allotted forty-five-minute time block. Jenae sealed the job offer when she assured Flynn that she was not planning on getting pregnant any time soon. Jenae was sold on the job when Flynn told her about quarterly retreats and a generous remuneration package, which included a company car.

"I'll need to confer with my boss, but as far as I am concerned, you're hired. If she approves, we'll send an offer letter soon and you can start training on the first of the month," Flynn said as he stood and walked Jenae to the door. She reached out her hand. "Oh yeah, you Yanks like to shake hands. I look forward to working with you." Flynn grabbed too hard, and shook too long, but Jenae didn't mind. She skipped to the parking lot and thought about living with her new husband in an apartment high in the sky.

Chapter 9

Eager Beavers

Logan

June Mink sat at the end of the bar at the *Eager Beaver* with her legs crossed with a red fuck-me-pump dangled off of her right foot. Her ankle moved in a circular motion when eligible men entered the establishment. She was the first girl Logan saw and he got an immediate stiffy imagining her clothes dangling from her glistening body. Two other girls sitting at the bar looked over their shoulder and winked at him. A small but imposing man with sunken eyes waved Logan over to the bar.

"You like these girls? Want to buy one a juice? They'll talk to you if you buy them juice. They're very thirsty, and their VD cards are good. They just got tested," the bartender asked, smiling with long yellow teeth.

"Sure, I like her." Logan pointed to June Mink.

"Yah, good choice. Ten dollars, please."

"And I'd like a Red Horse beer, too."

"That will be ten dollars and twenty-five cents."

June Mink reminded him of some of the girls he'd corresponded with by mail from his hideout trailer at Joshua Tree National Park. Her English was sparse but her body and hand gestures let him know that she was up for anything. She was an eager beaver because she wanted to get away from the boiling sleeping loft with a tin roof where the girls stayed when they weren't working. June only earned room and board as an employee, and tips from her johns. The bar owner occasionally gave a few dollars to her father when he came in and demanded a recruitment fee. June Mink's ultimate goal was to turn a john into a husband and take her and her family to a better life in a wealthy country.

June Mink thought she'd hit the jackpot when she walked into the Aussie's hotel room across the street. Logan handed her a glass of water. She placed it on the nightstand next to the bed and got to work.

"You like? You so sexy. You turn me on." June Mink rubbed his shoulders and moved her hands directly to his hardened cock.

"Yes, I like very much," Logan thought back on the last time he had sex. It cost him a lot more than ten bucks.

He rubbed his hands on her tiny nipples as he turned her around on the bed. She lifted her dress while Logan lowered her panties and massaged her ass while looking where he would plant his manhood.

"Ah, yeah baby," June Mink cried out dramatically as Logan spanked her and took his eighth and final pump.

Logan was in lust. His brown-eyed beauty was his for the week. A hundred-fifty-dollar bar fee was reasonable to keep June Mink as his girlfriend.

A week of wining and dining his sexy girlfriend came to an end when Logan awoke and found money missing from his wallet. June Mink took a vacation and Logan rethought his situation.

Nobody knows I'm alive – except Captain Bart – and he wishes me dead. My poor mom thinks I'm dead. How could I do that to her? My dad treated her like shit and then killed himself. I got my dad's genes. I'm a horrible person. All of the dastardly deeds I've done to others, I deserve to be dead like my dad. Nobody would know if I died now.

Logan threw his new purchases, including a boxed gold ring with a tiny diamond, into his duffel bag and checked out of the hotel. His lungs were tight, his eyes were watery and he had trouble exhaling. Smog was extra thick. He jumped over small piles of trash as he walked to the bus station. He saw an overweight woman wearing a house dress laid on her side in a wet gutter as he approached the ticket counter. Sirens sounded louder as an ambulance approached and bystanders stood over her. Logan flinched as his eyes darted back and forth between the buses lined up in the station and the approaching emergency vehicle. He lowered his head, raised his duffle bag and scurried to the counter to catch the next bus headed in the direction of his true love, Joy Lyn.

———◆———

It didn't take long to see the beauty of the countryside on the island. The bus stopped on a highway for one-way traffic because farmers spread rice crops on one side of the road to dry. Jeepneys and cars passed by slowly, careful not to disturb rice kernels. Jungles off the side of the road were lush with tall trees and vines, monkeys, pythons and wild boar.

"Hey, look at that monkey swinging in the trees. He's got big teeth," Logan pointed out the window as he looked back at his Caucasian seat mate wearing sunglasses and green cap.

"Yeah, there's a lot of crazy shit around here." He yawned and leaned his head back.

"I'm Logan, are you in the military?" Logan asked with a semi-convincing Aussie accent.

"What gives it away? I'm Steve by the way. Where's your accent from?"

"Ah, Australia mate; from Sydney. I'm here to meet up with my bride-to-be," Logan said.

"There's a lot of that going around here – especially with the uprisings in the government in the past year. Uncle Sam sent me here. It's a battle between civil rights and corrupt leaders. I'm not sure which side we are on," Steve said.

"Hopefully the right side." Logan added.

"We'll see. Local Filipinos mostly hate Americans right now. They get friendlier closer to military bases. We hire them to help add to the economy. Sitting next to another white guy makes me less of a target; we look like a joined force for now."

"Yeah, I hear they like Aussies and Kiwis better than Americans. I'm hoping to pick up some work on the docks or on a boat closer to my girl's hometown," Logan said.

"Make friends with the Negritos, they're the natives of these islands and they like white guys better than the Filipinos, and they're fierce. See that guy at the front? He's a Negrito. Just last month the Navy hired a group of them to find out who was stealing from the base and bring them to justice – you know like rakes and wire and stuff that was lying around in sheds on the base."

"Did they find them?" Logan asked.

"Apparently they found a half dozen guys who were in a theft gang and brought them back to the base. At dawn, my CO drove up to the gate and found six heads displayed on pikes over the fence line."

"Crikey! Did the Navy tell them to kill 'em?"

"Obviously not. I guess they got their communications mixed up. The Negrito language is difficult and their culture is definitely different from ours."

Headed west toward Olongapo, the bus met a rain storm and muddy, potholed roads. A detour caused by a downed tree over the highway navigated them on winding dirt roads through the jungle. Steve didn't seem concerned, so Logan relaxed and closed his eyes while he thought about his next moves to get closer to Joy Lyn with his best foot forward. He planned to settle around the Subic Bay Area and find work on the docks or on a boat.

Logan awoke to the feeling of the bus picking up speed and women shrieking. Rain came down in buckets as they careened down a mountain road. The bus driver slammed his brakes and they screamed back at him. A huge fat python slowly moved across their path and the driver tried his best to swerve to miss it even though the entire road was blocked by the log-sized serpent. A front left wheel bounced off of the enormous snake, flipped upside down and made a path through the jungle down the side of the mountain.

Screams from passengers ceased when they came to a stop in deep green wilderness. Gravity formed piles of groaning humans on the ceiling of the bus, painted with splatters of blood. Mildewed foliage outside the window took on the scent of diesel fuel. Logan regained consciousness as he heard the driver speaking to static on the radio. He wiped his face with the collar of his shirt and spit blood from his cut lip.

Steve groaned from beneath bodies and luggage. Logan checked on passengers as he pulled them off of him. He felt like a hero until he found an old man with a snapped neck.

"At least he didn't suffer," Logan mumbled as he found his black duffle and sat Steve up against the side of the coach. The bus made one more quarter turn as humanity began to move around inside the metal coffin.

"Open the hatch and get out!" the bus driver yelled in Tagalog and English.

Logan helped women and children out first, then Steve, then his duffle bag, and himself.

———•◆•———

Deep jungle plant life with rustling sounds in the trees and brush was the most difficult terrain imaginable. Logan continued down the mountain with his revolver in hand. Steve rested fifty-feet from the bus with a broken leg – a safe distance in case the gas tank blew up.

Logan decided to disappear in the jungle, and make his own way to avoid discovery by authorities when they showed up to rescue the others. It was a repeat of his own story: An offbeat man in an offbeat land. He had no friends or allies with only his instincts to survive and a desire to fit in.

Voices from above dissipated with every downward step. He was glad he wore boots. Leather between his ankle and a poisonous snake was his best defense against rotting in an undiscovered grave. He saw monkeys swinging in the canopy and his mind visited a memory of his seventh birthday. His mom and dad had taken him to the Cincinnati Zoo to celebrate.

Monkeys climbed man-made rope canopies and swung arm to leg to tail to arm to leg. One imp in particular was just as curious about Logan as Logan was about him. Logan spoke to the monkey, "oo, oo, oo." He started with a slow low pitch. When the monkey came nearer to watch, Logan said, "oo, oo, oo . . . oo, oo, oo, oo, ah, ah, ah, ah, AAH, AAH, AAH," the cadence got faster and louder with a high pitch ending in a primal scream. The monkey tilted his head at first but jumped erratically and hit the protective glass with a bang, and returned aggressive screams. Logan laughed out loud and pointed at the angry primate.

Loud rustling came from above and he heard a snort. "Shit!" Logan exhaled as he unzipped his duffle bag and checked the chamber of his revolver for bullets. He had just loaded it for the bus ride, but wanted to be sure it was properly armed. Muffled crackling stopped as his eyes darted back and forth scanning for movement. Without warning the ground trembled as a wild boar rumbled from above in his direction. Logan steadied his revolver with elbows bent as he looked down the barrel. A thousand-pound horned pork bullet charged at full speed. *Bang, bang, bang, bang!*

Chapter 10

Hagley Highrise

Jenae and Neve

Floor to ceiling windows met at the corners of a two-bedroom apartment high in the sky. The living room with a million-dollar view of Hagley Park featured an apricot, crushed-velvet sectional couch large enough for two visitors to sleep toe-to-toe. Jenae was proud of herself for finding it advertised in the paper and knew it was over-priced, but the apartment needed something grand to fit in. Neve had commissioned a craftsman to build a platform bed to fit their queen-sized mattress, and Jenae refinished a second-hand table and chairs that fit into a small dining area. Boxes of marketing materials sent from the pharmaceutical company mostly filled a small second bedroom.

She had spent two weeks in training on the North Island and had met her new best friend. Fiona was hired the same day as Jenae. The South Island was split geographically into North and South regions, and Jenae was assigned the north section, which included Christchurch. Fiona lived in Christchurch, but traveled to her sales area, which was acceptable as a single young lady. While in training, the young professionals bonded over learning about asthma medications and shared personal stories about growing up in very different lifestyles. Fiona was reared on a remote part of the South Island. Her father was a doctor and taught her how to fish off of their seaside property. She was homeschooled but eventually attended a university in Christchurch. Jenae had only heard about homeschooled kids in a weird way. Although Jenae was married, she mostly identified with single women with no children.

⸺◆⸺

"Hey, my sister and her husband want to go on a weekend away for their honeymoon. They want to know if we can watch the kids." Neve approached Jenae as she applied her make-up in the bathroom mirror.

"Sure, when? Why isn't your mum watching them? Doesn't she usually take care of them?"

"She can do it one night, but has plans with her new boyfriend. Yuck, I can't stand the thought of that. Anyway, they need help next weekend."

"I'm free as usual," Jenae said.

"The thing is, I've already scheduled a training flight on that Saturday, so you'd be on your own with the two wee ones all day," Neve said.

"OK, I'll do it. It's not like I have a social life without you," Jenae said.

"You can take them over to the park and feed them snacks. They take naps, too, so it shouldn't be hard," Neve assured.

"I can handle the kids, but aren't you supposed to be further along in your training? I thought you'd be picking up flying jobs by now."

Neve's ears turned red as he touched his forehead. "About that. I wanted to tell you sooner, but there was so much going on and I didn't want to worry you. You know . . . moving here, getting married. And you got a new job and went to training for a few weeks."

"What happened, Neve?" Jenae stood tall with her hands on her hips.

"I had my check ride almost two months ago and long story short, I failed it," Neve said in a weakened voice. "I thought I would have been able to reschedule it and have it done before you'd notice."

Jenae's eyebrows drew together and she faced Neve straight on. She looked straight into his eyes and held his hand. Neve looked away.

"Are you OK? Why didn't you just tell me? I'm sorry that you felt like you had to hide it from me," Jenae said.

"Do you still love me? I failed."

"Of course, I still love you. I don't love you because you will be a pilot someday. I love you for your character and commitment. You can always find something else to do if this doesn't work out," Jenae said.

"Well, you don't have to worry about that, I have another check ride scheduled and I'm positive that I will pass this one. Thanks for understanding. I thought you'd be mad."

"Maybe a little mad that you didn't tell me right off the bat. You owe me an ice cream scoop from the dairy, and a large bouquet of freesias."

The dairy around the corner from the high rise became a popular place when the niece and nephew came to visit. Lollies and freshly made ice cream saved Jenae from a certain meltdown of the kids on her weekend to watch them. She was determined to show her new in-laws and Neve that she would be a loving and caring mother. She wanted children badly, but wasn't sure how and when they would fit into her life.

The young boy had just learned to run, and bee-lined it to a babbling brook in Hagley Park with his ice cream cone in hand. His curly locks bounced as he giggled and looked back with a big smile at his sister and Aunt Jenae.

"NO!" Jenae screamed as she saw him approaching a steep embankment to rocks below in the stream. He paused and dropped his cone as Jenae caught up running with his sister tucked under her arm like a rugby ball. The boy squealed and took off again. Jenae reached her free arm out as he flew in the air toward certain injury and a visit to the emergency room. She caught him midair and the three of them slid down the embankment together on wet green grass. Jenae's running shoes stopped short of the stream, but her pants were skid marked with mud and grass stains and her elbow had road burn. The children remained unscathed except for melted ice cream on their chins.

"How was your day with the children?" Neve asked when he returned from flight training.

"Oh, it was great. We went to the park like you suggested. They were intrigued by the stream and are taking a nap in our bed right now." Jenae didn't want to let on that she was overtaxed with two children under her watch and felt comfortable keeping a secret about the near-plunge experience into icy shallow water.

⸻◆⸻

Her first week on the job visiting local doctors and telling them about the latest and greatest asthma medication seemed like a breeze. Jenae mapped out six doctors for everyday that week and called for appointments. Two signed up for lunch presentations and one more office of three general practitioners could meet her before office hours in the morning. She promised to bring scones, sausage rolls, fruit, sandwiches and a limited-edition calendar. Prints of photographs by Ansel Adams given by her company were a hot commodity in the medical community that quarter. At the first surgery she visited, a doctor studied black and white photographic images while gingerly lifting each page with care. *I should hand out white cotton gloves to enhance the experience,* Jenae thought.

<hr>

Fiona caught up with her at the end of the month for morning tea in central Christchurch. She had visited her doctors already for the week and wanted to debrief on what it was like to be a pharmaceutical sales rep.

"I'm not used to being dressed up all of the time. And I don't have any cool giveaways like you do – just some free samples," Fiona said as she added raw sugar to her cup of black tea.

"Yeah, I was surprised a calendar would get me into so many offices. They were really excited to get their hands on one. It must have been a big expense since they limited the number per office," Jenae said.

"Surgeries. Doctor offices are called surgeries here. Even though the doctors aren't surgeons," Fiona explained.

"I'm still learning. We may speak the same language, but it doesn't always mean the same thing. I've figured out that the cadence is most important for people to understand me."

"How are you doing driving on the left side of the road here?"

"Oh my goodness, it's not easy . . . especially when I'm driving down a road with no other cars and none are parked on the side of the road. I completely forget which side I should be on, and I find myself staying in the middle just in case."

"I'm not a great driver myself. I'd rather be riding my bike around, but I'd need a big satchel to carry all of the brochures," Fiona said.

"I'd probably get hit head on. I didn't tell you. I got a red-light ticket in the mail last week. So embarrassing. The company passed it on to me to pay."

"Oh no, there aren't too many of those around. You are the chosen one," Fiona chuckled.

"Well, I called the traffic office and explained that I'm American and that I just got here and the driver in front of me was at fault. They were intrigued and asked me to come in to explain the situation."

"I didn't know we had a traffic office. So how did it go? How much was the ticket?"

"The two officers that I met with were really nice. They had pictures of me stopped in the intersection when the light turned red. I pointed to the stupid woman in front of my car who wouldn't turn left because she was scared or something. Anyway, I was stuck in the intersection because of her."

"So, did they make you pay the ticket?"

"One officer had just returned from New York City and had done a ride along with the cops there. He had fun but was terrified the whole time and understood driving on the other side of the road was difficult. He said that he could never do it, especially in New York City. He let me off and dismissed the ticket. Yay!"

"Lucky you."

Making friends was never difficult for Jenae, but Fiona meant a lot to her. She relied on Fiona's kindness and genuine nature to help assimilate into a new culture.

Chapter 11

Docks and Cocks

Logan

It was as if chickens and roosters called him down the mountain jungle into town. A rooster stood at a clearing near a road below, *Cock-a-doodle doo!* He was calm and commanding, imposing and strong, which reminded Logan of the attitude of Filipino people. At that moment, Logan thought of himself more like a rooster. A rooster can stand against strong winds and can withstand pressure from other roosters. They have resilience to recover quickly from any form of difficulty and hardship. Logan had just saved his own life again . . . by emptying his gun on a charging boar. He had proven to himself that he still had the will to live; tested by times of crisis and challenges.

Logan swabbed decks of boats and hoisted nets for any fishing outfit that would hire him. He wanted to establish himself as a hardworking man committed to marrying a sweet woman, Joy Lyn, and had made contact with her by postcard from his semi-permanent residence near the docks.

No response was expected, but at least she knew where to find him until Logan worked up the nerve to face her father to ask for a courtship and eventual marriage. His goal was to buy a fishing boat and learn the industry before he asked for Joy Lyn's hand in marriage.

Joy Lyn held the postcard to her heart after she read it. Her stomach fluttered with butterflies as she thought about the possibilities of marrying a man from the United States. She didn't know he'd been hiding under an Australian facade. A newlywed military couple that she worked for on base were friendly and generous and she wanted to be like them. Joy Lyn took off work early after the lady of the house offered her an early start on the weekend with full pay. She couldn't get the thought of Logan out of her head and kept the postcard in her purse. Knowing that he was only one town over from her work, she had to see him, and could get away with extra time before she was expected back home.

A Jeepney headed in the direction of the docks had one seat available for Joy Lynn to wedge into. She was one of two young ladies on the dusty ride to the ocean, and the only person who held onto a scapular hung around her neck. The Miraculous Medal, with Mary standing on a globe with a snake beneath her feet on one side and two hearts representing Mary and Jesus on the other, was a precious gift given to her for confirmation in the Catholic Church. Her mother and father had bestowed the family heirloom to her as the oldest daughter, and she ran her fingers over the surface to calm her nerves.

Logan had finished a full day out on a fishing boat and smelled worse than a truck driver and an oil field worker combined. Fish, saltwater and body odor were more than even he could bear. Logan never worked so hard in his life, but never felt so satisfied. A rubber hose attached to a community spigot delivered a refreshing cold shower next to his one room accommodation. He had a bucket of suds and a sponge to scrub dirt and grime from bodily crevasses. A mattress and soiled pillow just inside the door of his apartment looked inviting, but his stomach rumbled and forced him to find dinner at the local shopping area.

The Jeepney stopped long enough for Joy Lyn to hop off at the closest street near the address on Logan's postcard. She smiled, waved and straightened her knee-length skirt. Her long black hair was unleashed from being tied up on the windy ride to the coast. As she ran her fingers through her hair like a comb to untangle her silky locks, an overwhelming gust of fish smell wafted her way. Staring at the address and surveying street names, she pulled a picture out of her purse of the sandy-haired man from California. She had studied Logan's face for so long that it was burned into her brain, but wanted to be sure she could identify him in real life. She made her way closer to the address on the postcard and stopped in her tracks. There it was, a door in a row of tenements with his address, "102." She stood before it and knocked softly, praying that he'd answer. Her soft knuckles knocked louder with no answer and she pounded her fist against the door as if she was raiding the place, just in case he was asleep inside. Still no answer. Joy Lyn's shoulders slumped slightly as she lowered her head and closed her eyes.

Walking back to the main road, she smelled roast pork and saw smoke wafting from an outdoor shopping area. She could at least bring back something for dinner to her family since she just got paid her weekly wage with a little bonus on top.

Joy Lyn lived up to her name and always saw the sunny side of life. She didn't know any better. A sandy-haired man sat at an outdoor table faced away from her. She pulled the picture from her pocket and slowly circled the man drinking a local beer with an empty paper plate with a few fermented vegetables left over.

Logan turned his head to the right when he saw something in his peripheral vision. Joy Lyn stopped, stared and slowly lifted the picture to examine his face. She smiled shyly and spoke with a shaky voice,"

"Logan? Are you Logan?"

Logan jumped slightly and felt a tightness in his eyes as he blinked rapidly. He surveyed the road behind Joy Lyn and stood up to greet her.

"Are you Joy Lyn? Oh, my God. Are you Joy Lyn? How did you find me? I was waiting..."

"For what silly. We're in the same country," Joy Lyn grabbed his hands, smiled and looked fixedly up at his sunburned face.

"Please, sit down. What can I get for you to eat? Do you want a beer?" Logan stumbled over his words in a high-pitched voice.

"Here, let me get that." Logan pulled out a metal chair at his table and dusted off the seat before Joy Lyn sat down with a smile.

"I can't believe you are right in front of me." Joy Lyn's heart filled with butterflies. He was still the man she wanted.

The penpals giggled and gazed at each other. She was mesmerized by Logan's intense stare and how he raised his left eyebrow with the start of every sentence. His right eyebrow was fixed and higher than the normal brow line and he had a red mark from a pimple in the crease of the left side of his nose. He kept his hands folded in a ball on the cafe table and stuck out his tongue when thinking of an answer. Joy Lyn wasn't shy with Logan because he had made her feel like she was the only girl for him in his letters. She answered all of his questions.

"What do you like most about living in the Philippines?" Logan asked.

"I don't know. Probably my family. We are very close, and as the oldest daughter I feel responsible to take care of my younger siblings and parents when they get older. That's why I want to stay in my country."

"How old's your dad?"

"He's in his forties, but he looks and acts younger."

"Oh wow, he must have been young when you were born."

"Well, twenty-four or something like that."

"At least I'm in my thirties. Not quite your dad's age. How does he feel about you dating?"

"He knows I have been writing to you, but he's very protective and very religious. He only wants me to be courted by a man who is serious about marriage. Do you go to church?" Joy Lyn asked.

"I've been to church, but to be honest, not in a long time. I'm willing to try, though. Will that count?" Logan tilted his head and raised his left eyebrow.

"Maybe you can come to Mass with me sometime." Joy Lyn wrote down the name of her parish and the time, "11 AM" on a napkin and tucked it into Logan's t-shirt pocket. She looked at her watch and realized that two hours had passed in a flash and her father would be expecting her home soon. "I gotta go."

"When can I see you again?" Logan asked.

"Check your pocket." Joy Lyn blew Logan a kiss as she skipped off toward the smell of meat roasting on a large open grill.

"I'm glad you found me! I miss you already." Logan stood up and waved as he leaned against a table and watched as Joy Lyn disappeared around the street corner.

Logan was certain that he would marry Joy Lyn. She glowed like an angel in the sunset as she walked away. Men know these things.

Chapter 12

Road Warrior and Jet Setter

Jenae and Neve

The two sides of traveling for work were extreme. Jenae loved getting out into the countryside of the South Island; her favorite new experiences were eating fresh seafood, watching sheep corralled down a paved highway, and the first glance of a glacier lake while driving through the mountains. However, she missed Neve during her week away. They only talked briefly before bed while she traveled, and she felt lonely all by herself in a different hotel room every night.

"So, who'd you meet with today?" Neve graciously acted interested.

"Who didn't I meet with? You know me, I'm so competitive, I'm determined to put a check next to every doctor on my roster. Some haven't been visited in three years! One guy had never been seen."

"I bet they're excited to interact with someone from civilization. It's pretty remote where you are, isn't it?"

"Yep. If I would have gotten a flat tire, I don't know what I would've done. I drove through the mountains today to get to a guy that other reps have been afraid to visit."

"Why? Is he scary, or is it just too far off the beaten path?"

"Rumor has it that he got out of prison a few years ago for killing his wife. That's why no company rep would visit that doctor; not even the other divisions. He spent twelve years in prison, but now he's out, the government planted him in the middle of nowhere for the few patients that live out here."

"Oh my God, Jenae. Why would you go visit that guy? It's too dangerous," Neve said.

"I told you that I took it as a personal challenge to give this doctor our marketing materials. Some poor hunter out here could have an asthma attack and not know about our medication. Plus, it was a huge check off of my list today. Flynn will be impressed."

"Obviously you got out of there alive, but what was he like?"

"He was mild mannered. Nothing odd stood out except his surgery was in the middle of nowhere and he didn't have a receptionist. The office was dark because it was nestled in a stand of trees. He seemed pleased to have a visitor and extra pleased that I was American. I unloaded a bunch of marketing materials on him to last him another couple of years."

"That's it? He didn't have a gun on his lap or cyanide pills in a bottle on his desk?"

"No, in fact I commented on a photograph of him and a woman on his shelf. He said that was his new wife. I don't know, maybe it was self-defense."

"Well, be careful," Neve said.

Jenae looked out the window of her motel room on the ground level.

"Oh crap, a couple of Kea birds are pecking at the rubber on my windshield wipers. I need to shew them off the bonnet of the car. I'll call you tomorrow. Love you!" Jenae said.

"Good luck, and like I said, be careful. Those buggers can be feisty."

"Nighty pies." Jenae made kissing noises into the phone.

⊷◆⊶

While Jenae was away, Neve could concentrate all of his attention on painting a flip house with his brother, and studying for his next check ride. He got in some of his best mental chair-flying while mindlessly rolling fresh paint onto walls. He visualized the terrain on a blank wall and filled it in at a steady pace, recalling altitudes and airspeeds around mountains down to the ocean below. A check ride was scheduled for Thursday, while Jenae was away working on the West Coast. He wanted to surprise her by passing his cross-country certification, or pretend like it didn't happen if he failed. Implications for passing this check ride were enormous. If he passed, it meant that he would be able to get a real job flying small planes and make some money while he accumulated flying hours to get a wide body rating one day.

He planned to fly to Auckland and back in one day. Neve showed up early to the airport hangar with a fresh haircut, new dress pants and a conservative collared shirt. He took his aviator sunglasses off when he entered the briefing room and was relieved to see that he was the first one there. It gave him time to turn on a kettle of water for a cup of tea. While it heated, he sat in a wooden chair, closed his eyes and began to think of nothing. He cleared his mind before visualizing the entire flight to Auckland with his evaluator. He even visualized a nice lunch at the airport cafe before loading up the plane and flying back to Christchurch. Just as he successfully landed the virtual plane in his mind, he heard the outside door slam. Neve rubbed his eyes and stood to greet his instructor.

"Good morning, sir. It's nice to see you again." Neve said.

"It certainly is. It's been a few months since your first instrument check ride fail. I see that you passed it with a more forgiving evaluator."

"I suppose. But you taught me invaluable lessons in my first attempt, so thanks for that," Neve brown nosed.

"Auckland airport is my favorite lunch spot. Maybe you can buy me a steak sandwich when we land," the instructor half-heartedly joked."

"Yeah, yeah, sounds like a plan. Anyway, I checked the weather up there and right now the airport is socked in with fog, but by the time we get there we should have well over five miles visibility and two-thousand foot ceilings or better on approach. If not, our alternate today is the Ohakea Airport (NZOH) to the south of Auckland. The tower is reporting strong crosswinds over the Cook Straight as usual. The plane is fueled for the flight time to Auckland plus a forty-five minute reserve." Neve handed the evaluator a clipboard with the flight plan and pointed to the fueling and emergency airport data. Neve filed his flight plan and the pair headed to the small red plane parked outside of the hangar. Neve walked with wide steps and a steady gait to inspect the aircraft, starting at the front propeller. He ducked under the right wing and ran his hand over the body of the plane as he eyeballed the undercarriage.

"Alright Neve, it looks like you are prepared for the IFR (Instrument Flight Rules) flight up to Auckland. On return back to Christchurch, you will be using VFR (visual flight rules)."

"Roger that."

The planning sheet had specific taxi routes for runways in Christchurch and Auckland. In addition, the flight sheet read:

-KIWI01, Cessna 175, NZCH (0000)

-NO180 F 080 DCT CH H110 NS H252 NP H384AA

-NZAA 0120 NZOH

Shortly before starting the engines, Neve called on the radio to get the departure clearance (Standard instrument departure, route of the flight, altitude clearance and transponder code 3443).

Neve released the brake and used foot pedals to steer the small Cessna to the end of the runway. His shoulders were back, his chest out and his chin high as he scanned for landing traffic and to verify he was on the correct runway. Skies were clear with a few light clouds and the sun was low, shining brightly off of the reflection of his sunglasses.

The flight to Auckland was every bit what Neve had planned and expected. He hit every beat of the flight plan and answered every question before the evaluator had a chance to ask it. Temptation to relax was strong because Neve knew he'd nailed the first leg of his exam. But he knew his evaluation would continue through lunch, and made an extra effort to be attentive and kind to the airport workers and waitress at the restaurant.

"This steak sandwich is just as juicy as I remember it. How do you like yours, Neve?"

"Delicious, thanks for recommending it," Neve said before sinking his teeth into another bite of medium rare sirloin.

"What are your aviation plans from here?"

"Ah, well, I'd like to fly commercial for one of the major airlines. I have the urge to travel the world and that's one way to do it."

"How does your wife feel about that? It takes a strong woman to hold down the household and raise children on her own while you are out working on trips." The evaluator looked directly into Neve's eyes as he sipped on a cup of tea.

"Strong is one thing my wife is. She's American you know, and they breed 'em with a different mindset there. I think she could handle it; she may even like her independence while I'm gone."

"American, huh? That opens your options up a lot for international flying. In fact, I know a few blokes who commute to the U.S. from New Zealand. I can put you in touch with them," the evaluator offered.

"Aw, yeah! That would be amazing. I'd love to get back to America and get in with a big carrier there."

"You shouldn't have any trouble getting a green card. You're married to a Yank."

"You wouldn't think so, but I was dealing with a government guy who strung me up by the balls last time I applied to stay in America. Hopefully he's out of the way now."

The evaluator hit the can while Neve paid for lunch at the register.

— ◆ —

On the flight back to Christchurch, Neve identified landmarks to orient himself while flying VFR. He started his flight at 5,500 feet out of Auckland. As he headed south, he stayed on the west coastline of the North Island with North Plymouth in his sights. The plane then flew east and crossed over at Whanganui to just west of Wellington and over the Cook Straight to the eastern coastline of the South Island over Kaikoura. He saw whales breaching below in deep waters just off the shore. Neve checked in with ATIS for proper orientation for landing and his heart dropped when they reported strong crosswinds at Christchurch airport. He rubbed the sweat off of his right palm onto his pant leg and took a deep breath before focusing on his landing checklist. The evaluator sat in silence with his head forward while observing Neve's every move.

"Two thousand, fifteen hundred, one thousand feet," Neve spoke out loud.

"Landing gear down, runway one in sight, eight hundred, six hundred, four hundred, two hundred," Neve continued as the wings began to tilt up and down.

Neve took in a calm breath through his nose and set the plane down as he exhaled with barely a noise from the wheels on the runway.

Chapter 13

Love and Joy Lyn

Logan

Sailing on a fishing boat was freeing and cleared Logan's mind. Fresh breezes off of the water filled his lungs with hope. It gave him time to think about all of the terrible deeds he'd committed for his own satisfaction and to think about his future with Joy Lyn. He wished he could get the letters back that he had sent to Jenae in San Francisco before he boarded the plane that fateful night. He was conflicted between wanting to see her again to apologize for stalking her and trying to poison her, and wanting her to believe that he was dead.

Joy Lyn was the focus for his future, but he still his fantasies had it worked out with Jenae. She escaped his grasp, but he kept her locked in his memory, especially when he pleasured himself at night.

Pepe and Margarita were proud that their daughter had found a foreigner to marry. Joy Lyn went along with Logan's charade that he was an Australian and not an American. She didn't care where he was from as long as he was willing to stay in the Philippines with her to raise a family. He'd promised her a big house in a gated community nearby after they married.

Logan attended the Catholic Church with Joy Lyn and her family every Sunday when he was on dry land. He stood and kneeled when the congregation did and spoke prayers and creeds out loud, but hadn't yet taken communion. He attended adult conversion classes when he could and knew that he wouldn't get Pepe's blessing for marriage until he was baptized and confirmed into the church.

As long as he wasn't officially engaged, Logan could justify visits to strip clubs and occasional dates with prostitutes, because Joy Lyn was as pure as an angel and saving herself for marriage. His thighs would chafe if he walked around with blue balls for six months. Pepe was clear that adultery was against the law in the Philippines, and many men had been jailed for the offense. Pepe also emphasized that jail would be too light of a sentence for anyone who cheated on his daughter.

Joy Lyn saw the consequences of unintended pregnancies first hand every time she volunteered for the nuns at the orphanage near the base. Many children were half American and half Filipino, and the result of paid sex from strip clubs. Even though it was a large compound, it was a secret in plain sight. Tall walls surrounded a home for the children, while guards protected the gates. The family that Joy Lyn worked for collected basic need products for the children and delivered them once a month on a Sunday after church. Joy Lyn was the go-between because foreigners weren't allowed inside the gates. Disease swiftly passed through the residents, and tuberculosis was especially contagious and debilitating. After church, Joy Lyn asked her priest what the children most needed in the orphanage so that she could relay it to her employer.

"God will provide," was the only thing he said.

———◆———

U.S. aircraft often flew overhead as the fishing boat headed out for deeper water. Logan had agreed to a full week stint on a kumpit ship to move trading goods between islands. Two small boats tied behind slowed them down and kept Logan busy until each was delivered.

During the week, a military aircraft went missing on a routine training mission in the fathomless waters where deep-sea fishing boats dared to venture. Locals gossiped that a lady pilot had been missing for a few days and she was presumed dead. Rescue efforts had been a bust and no wreckage had been found. Her husband had been interviewed on military newscasts and he was convinced that she was still alive. He felt her presence, and asked for prayers for her survival and for all of those searching for her.

At the end of a long week of loading goods on and off of the boat, Logan rested on a whirl of tightly wound ropes at the front of the ship. The back of his head lightly tapped the side of the wheel house as the captain swung his craft in the direction of home dock. Sun rays glimmered brightly off of the surface of the ocean, which caught Logan's attention. Everyone on the boat had their eyes out for the missing Air Force jet that week, but Logan felt he would be the hero to find the pilot. He needed to be a hero.

He jumped to his feet and waved his arms over his head. "I see her! Hey, I see her on the wing. Look!" Logan pointed to the horizon, at the pilot lost at sea, lying on a piece of her plane floating in calm waters. She was prone with her head covered by a helmet.

The captain swiftly turned the ship in her direction and alerted the crew to prepare for a rescue. A small row boat towed behind was prepared with life jackets, blankets and a jug filled with fresh water. As they approached, the captain yelled, "look for movement! Is she alive? Prepare for resuscitation and grab the stretcher."

The crew stood at the bow of the ship while Logan prepared the rowboat at the stern. He donned a life vest and paddle and was ready to launch when the captain gave him the go ahead.

"This is the closest I can get. Release the line and shove off. Logan and two other crew members paddled to the floating wreckage. The person on top was clearly a U.S. pilot, but she showed no movement. Waters remained calm as they quietly sculled closer to the debris. Logan reached out to turn the body over, and as he touched the back of her flight suit, he saw a pinky finger on her right hand move.

"She's alive!"

Pepe listened intently as Logan recalled events from rescuing the lost female pilot. Pepe knew her husband and respected him because he was strong and resolute for his children and for the military community during the uncertainty of her well-being. It was all Pepe heard over the past week, while he worked on base trimming bushes and cutting grass for airmen. Tension was high, and when Logan and the crew found the female pilot alive, a wave of relief washed over troops from both local bases. Pepe's future son-in-law had noble qualities. The boat crew were publicly named as local heroes for finding and rescuing her.

"Congratulations, Pepe. We are indebted to your future son-in-law." A local resident stopped on the side of the road to chat.

"Thank you! I'll pass that on to him. He's a fine man indeed," Pepe responded as he loaded fronds into the back of his work truck.

"We're so grateful that he and the boat crew were in the right place at the right time."

"Divine timing, I suppose. It was also fortunate that there was a ship nearby to care for the pilot and quickly get her to the hospital."

"Indeed. When is the wedding?"

"Soon, we are hoping sometime after Christmas. It will be a joyous union."

Any concerns that Pepe had about his daughter marrying Logan were wiped out and Pepe gave his blessing to marry Joy Lyn. Logan had proved that he was a stand up man and would take good care of his first daughter.

<hr>

Joy Lyn and Logan attended an engagement encounter at a weekend retreat to get to know each other on a deeper level. Both were nervous, but held hands as they entered the doors of the spiritual life center. Most couples on the retreat were Catholic and already engaged. Logan was neither, but the priest suggested that he and Joy Lyn attend the weekend to decide if marriage was a good plan for them. Both wanted children and agreed that they would be raised in the Catholic Church.

In group sessions, other couples were a good barometer of their commitment to one another. Sister Connie led a discussion on finances and role expectations in the home. Joy Lyn was comfortable being a boat captain's wife and looked forward to living on the waterfront.

Father Tom challenged the group to maintain sexual abstinence until marriage. Joy Lyn blushed and looked at her toes when he brought the subject up and couples talked openly about their sex life. It wasn't an issue for Joy Lyn, being a twenty-one-year-old virgin. She believed Logan when he told her that he had only a few sexual encounters and had remained celibate since he'd arrived in the Philippines.

The Sacrament of Marriage was front and center at the retreat. Logan knew little about sacraments, but he knew he had an obligation to remain faithful and to always honor and support his wife. Joy Lyn's heart opened up to Logan and she promised herself to commit to being the best wife and mother – for Logan and her future children, but mostly for herself.

He learned about Joy Lyn's upbringing and the history of her family. Logan had trouble sharing complete truths about his dysfunctional family, but he did show her the scar hidden in his hair line on the right side of his head.

"My father had a temper. He drank a lot and suffered from mental illness," Logan looked down.

"Oh no, I'm so sorry Logan. How did you get that scar?"

"I think it was an accident, but my dad just lost it one day when I was two years old or so and whacked me upside the head. I don't remember it."

Joy Lyn parted his hair with her dainty fingers and inspected the jagged scar.

"It looks like it's about seven centimeters long. That's big for a toddler's head."

"You may have noticed that the side of my forehead doesn't move either. I assume it has nerve damage. I try not to think about it because when I do, my heart hurts and my stomach turns in knots." Logan stood up and wiped his eyes. He'd never gone to therapy and knew the engagement encounter didn't serve that purpose, but Logan felt a release off of his shoulders.

Communication was a tough nut to crack for two people from different cultures and languages. Learning about religion was another added twist for Logan, but he looked forward to each class. He felt more understood by Joy Lyn and learned about himself as well. He learned that love notes went a long way in winning Joy Lyn's heart. She told him how much joy it brought her when she read his handwriting.

The weekend ended with prayer and reflection time. Newly married couples attended a final Mass with the group and answered questions of participants one-on-one. Logan felt validated when Joy Lyn read out loud a letter that her godmother and godfather sent in support of their relationship.

Chapter 14

Lake Taupo

Jenae and Neve

Six months of work at the pharmaceutical company flew by. It was easy compared to caring for patients twelve hours at a time in the hospital, but also challenging because she was in a foreign country. Less than a month after receiving a brand-new company car, Jenae crunched the right fender when she turned too close to a utility pole as she pulled into Helen's driveway.

"It's a good thing the company is impressed with your work, Jenae," Flynn chuckled on the phone when Jenae broke the news to her boss.

"They like my work?"

"You're setting records with visits and you are the quickest to crash our newest company car. Oh, and you got a traffic ticket in record time too."

"Oh my God. I'm so embarrassed. Driving on the other side of the road presents special challenges. I'm usually a really good driver."

"No worries. I'll set up a rental vehicle for you and let you know which body shop to drop off your car. Is it drivable?"

"Yes. It's not that bad. I'll have Neve take me to the airport for our quarterly retreat. That should save a few bucks on the rental car."

"Good thinking. I'll see you this weekend. It should be a really fun retreat; you're athletic, right? Bring boots and a swimsuit. I suppose you don't have a wetsuit."

"No wetsuit. Can't wait. Thanks for understanding, Flynn!"

"And don't forget to get a fifteen-minute presentation together. I sent a slide deck of photos to you. My team needs to impress the consultants coming in for the week."

━◆◆◆━

Neve walked off the elevator as he straightened out a stack of white envelopes that he picked up from the postbox in the lobby. He shoved the keychain in his jeans front pocket after he unlocked the front door of their high-rise condo. Jenae jumped up to greet him with a big hug and a kiss. Their eyes locked as she folded her hands around the back of his neck and kissed his lips in a series of pecks – she didn't mind his torn t-shirt at the collar and his paint-stained pants.

"How was your day? Are you getting to the end of the renovation on the flip property?"

"We should be able to stage it this weekend and get it on the market." Neve kissed her back and stopped in the kitchen to wash his hands and fingernails up to his elbows, like a surgeon scrubbing in for an operation.

"Let's go out and celebrate before I have to go to the North Island for work this weekend," Jenae said.

"I don't know, Jenae, I'm still waiting on my flight certificate so I can stop working construction and start flying for a paycheck. I think I passed, but I haven't received confirmation yet. I swore that I did well, but I had the same evaluator that flunked me on my first ride."

"Have you looked at the mail from today yet?"

"Yep, I flipped through, didn't see anything."

"Here, let me look." Jenae grabbed the stack of mostly bills and junk mail. Neve kicked his shoes off, laid back on a couch pillow and closed his eyes.

"Hey, what's this? Your name and address is handwritten . . . it's from Aviation Associates."

Neve popped up and his eyes widened. The white envelope had been stuck in a grocery circular. He picked at the edge of the letter and slid his finger under a glued flap to tear it open.

A one-page tri-folded letter on a printed letterhead started with the words, "Congratulations, you passed." Neve jumped up with a whoop, bent over and covered his face. Jenae grabbed the letter to read the gist of the entire letter.

"Yay! I'm so proud of you! You did it!" Jenae hugged Neve from behind while he wiped tears from his eyes.

"We did it. I couldn't have done it without your support." Neve turned around and held her with his strong arms.

"Well thank you, but you know that isn't true. You did all of the work and persevered," Jenae said.

"Let the celebration begin!"

Neve dropped Jenae and Fiona off at the front curb of the airport, not long after sunrise. Fiona's apartment was on the way to the airport and she took every opportunity to save money. A week of airport parking was expensive. As a single lady, she enjoyed the privacy and independence of her own place, but was ready to find a husband for love and convenience.

They were off to Lake Taupo for a pharmaceutical semi-annual meeting with big wigs and to team build in challenging wilderness. Gerald, a Wellington based pharmaceutical representative, picked the ladies up at the airport and they were off to Lake Taupo. Chauffeuring colleagues in the company car was an easy "yes" as long as it got him out of a day of doctor visits.

"How did your flight go, ladies? It was an early start for you, I gather."

"Good and uneventful," Jenae said.

Is it alright if we make a stop before we head out of town? I've got to check in some supplies at a warehouse," Gerry asked.

"Sure, you're driving. I hope you don't mind if I doze off while you drive," Fiona said.

Thirty minutes into the drive, they pulled up at a large metal roofed barn in the middle of a field. Boxes were stacked under an overhang, in front of the structure.

"Come on in, I'll show you around. It'll take me a few minutes to dolly these packages inside, but I want to show you what I've been working on," Gerry said.

The ladies changed into their hiking boots that Flynn had recommended for the week. The ground was muddy in between small flax shrubs. Ducks flew over a small pond glistening behind the barn. As they entered the threshold through large opened doors, Gerry gestured his arms toward his project and shouted, "Ta da!"

It was an elegant thirty-foot schooner constructed with teak wood with a large sail mast.

"What's this? A fancy boat?" Jenae asked.

"Yeah, I built it from scratch," Gerry said proudly. "I'm almost done with it after a few more coats of varnish. That's what I brought in on the dolly. I got a buyer for it a few months ago. It will be ready for the summer season."

"How long have you been working on it?" Fiona asked.

"A couple of years. It started as a passion project. I love working with wood and my dad and uncle taught me how to build boats. I built a boat with them that I kept and sail by myself. But this one is all me."

"Wow, what an accomplishment! I didn't know you could build a boat like this all by yourself," Fiona said.

"Like I said, it's a passion. I love the beauty of teak wood and its resilience, that's why it has a reputation for boat building over the centuries. I feel connected to past generations," Gerry said.

"You are a gifted craftsman! I grew up around boats on the coast and this is the most beautiful vessel that I've seen. I would love to ride on your boat sometime," Fiona gushed.

"Well, thank you. I can take you out on the water sometime. This one actually floats and sails well. My dad and I took it out for a test run last week." Gerry had a sparkle in his eye when he talked to Fiona.

—◇—

The crew of three hopped back into the car and cranked up the defroster and heater.

"It's cold for a spring day, isn't it?" Jenae asked as a cold spit of rain hit the windshield.

"It can get that way," Gerry said. "By the way, we're picking up another rep in the next town. She lives out here while her husband builds a house about twenty kilometers away. She asked if we can stop by his build to drop dinners off for him since she's going to be gone. There isn't a grocery nearby, and I guess no kitchen in the house yet either."

"Wow, you all are builders on the North Island aren't you?" Jenae asked.

"Somebody's gotta do it," Gerry said.

"I never thought of that. In America, most homes are built by big construction companies. But, my father-in-law was a home builder, so it makes a lot of sense," Jenae contemplated aloud.

It had been a long day by the time the reps made it to the retreat site at a lakeside resort. Jenae and Fiona were put in a room together in the women's cabin. Jenae picked the twin bed next to the inside wall, while Fiona agreed to take the bed next to a drafty sliding glass door. Little time remained to clean up and get to dinner at the main lodge.

Flynn was first to greet his reps at the lodge, seated up front at the bar drinking a beer with a full head of foam.

"Welcome, ladies. You are just in time for dinner, follow me. I think there'll be wine at the tables since you missed cocktail hour. How was your trip?"

"It was an adventure. We got to see interesting parts of the countryside. Did you know that Gerry builds boats?" Jenae asked.

"Yeah, yeah. Did you see his current project? Isn't it brilliant?" Flynn asked.

"He took us by the barn to have a look. I can't believe he's so talented with his hands," Fiona said.

"By the way, did you get your presentations prepared? If not, you'll need to work on them tonight. We have a full day of activities planned tomorrow and for the next two days we'll be presenting to the corporate gents who are here with us," Flynn said as he guided them into the dinner hall.

"I've got mine, but I'll look over it tonight, before bed," Jenae affirmed.

"Good on ya." Flynn gave her a squeeze on her shoulder.

Jenae enjoyed seeing colleagues that she met during orientation over the winter and met more senior employees for the first time. After dinner the lead marketing director presented team building exercises that would start early in the morning starting with abseiling off of a bridge and whitewater rafting. Fiona's eyes popped from fear by the announcement, but Jenae was excited to try something new.

⸺◆⸺

A night of tossing and turning under heavy wool blankets didn't affect Jenae's energy level for the adventures of the day. After breakfast, a gray bus with a red stripe down the side drove the group through the woods and stopped at a trailhead near an ornamental concrete bridge over a river. Three rafts were grounded on the river bank below. Guides looked up and smiled and waved to the group leaning over the edge, "Come on and join us!"

Another guide on the bridge gave instructions and demonstrated how to put on a harness and operate the rope system that would suspend them under the bridge as they descended.

"This is called abseiling. Anyone ever done this before?" the guide asked.

"Ah, I've done it a ton of times. It's easy," Flynn chimed in.

"Alright then, do you want to go first?"

"Hell yeah," Flynn said as he stepped into a harness and pulled it up to his waist.

The group was close to fifty-fifty men and women. All of the men pushed to the front of the line along the bridge and watched as Flynn elegantly lowered himself to a raft in the middle of the river waiting below. They each lowered down without incident, so Jenae wasn't worried about falling into the river. She was the first woman in line to attempt the descent and didn't think twice about the challenge. However, when she looked back at her female coworkers huddled together, she noticed three of them crying.

"What's wrong?" Jenae asked.

"I can't do it! We can't do it! I can't swim and I'm afraid of falling to my death."

"Ah, it'll be alright. We're strapped in, and you control the speed with the rope. It looks easy, watch, here I go."

Jenae stepped over the bridge guard rail and sat down over the water in mid air. She held the rope in her right hand and looked over her left shoulder to the guide with his arms up in the raft below. She let out short bursts of line which jerked her about every foot and a half. Finally, when she felt comfortable with the sturdiness of the apparatus, she released the rope in one steady motion and felt like a navy seal lowering out of a helicopter into a dangerous war zone. She giggled when her feet hit the raft and the guide helped release her from her harness.

"That was amazing!" Jenae yelled up to her co-workers leaning over the bridge. One woman still cried as she held her stomach and bent over in a yakking position. Flynn had climbed back to the top of the embankment to check on the ladies and tried to coax them over the edge. All but two completed the task. Some closed their eyes and whimpered, but most made it with a sense of pride.

Flynn bit his tongue as he held his hand out to help a member of his team into the raft from the bank of the river. He was kind about her not being able to complete the challenge, but Jenae could feel his irritated energy. It matched hers. The idea that people would be afraid of that task was unreasonable to her.

◆

From the front of the boat, Jenae was mesmerized by swirly white water ahead. Each team member took a turn at the back and steered while barking orders which way to paddle. Flynn imparted managerial wisdom while his minions were trapped with no way out.

"The purpose of our rafting trip is to learn to trust one another and to figure out leadership styles. We just had a demonstration of who was fearless enough to abseil off of a bridge into this boat. I was encouraged by all of your efforts."

"Ugh, what is that stench!"

"It smells like a rotting carcass," Flynn said.

"Gross, the wind is blowing it our way. It's getting worse," Jenae said.

"Ah, I see it. There's a dead cow on that bank on the right side."

As they paddled downwind from the rotting cow, Jenae took her turn as captain. The sun had come out and warmed her skin.

"OK, Jenae. What's your leadership style? How should we paddle?" Flynn asked.

"I guess it depends on what mood I'm in. We are past the rocks and white water and dead animals, so I say we each watch the river and make adjustments on an individual basis. I trust all of you to keep us from capsizing. I'm just going to close my eyes and soak up the sun. We'll be fine," Jenae said.

Chapter 15

Scary Scot

Jenae

The first day of the retreat adventure was in the books and two were yet to follow, but evening time was reserved for downloading stories and sharing laughs. A group of photographic slides had been given to each member of Flynn's team a month in advance and were the backdrop for orations based on experiences as pharmaceutical representatives with the company. The same photo deck was used for each presentation and was an indicator of each rep's personality.

A cerebral chap talked about numbers and sales figures related to his products. Two reps were emotional as they talked about their families and self-discovery.

Flynn leaned over to Jenae and whispered into her ear after her South Island cohort's presentation, "damn, I was worried that Walt was going to come out of the closet and make an announcement that he was gay. We all know it, but this isn't the venue to shout it out to the world."

"He came pretty close! I think he was tearing up," Jenae said.

"OK Jenae, it's your turn to present. You do have something don't you?" Flynn nagged.

"Yes, I do. It's not like the other presentations, but I'll give it a go." Jenae worried that her American sense of humor wouldn't translate well to New Zealanders.

She had prepared a comedy act based on Late Night TV host David Letterman's "Top Ten" routine. With her ten slides she ribbed a different person from the company with each one. Her timing was spot on and she heard uncomfortable chuckles and saw eyes darting back and forth with each click of the slide show button. She hadn't seen the big wigs from corporate including the president slip into the back of the darkened room. Half way through comedy digs on her workmates, she heard roaring laughter from the back. Her final slide dug the deepest on her manager, Flynn. He cried with laughter in concert with the audience and was honored to be her biggest laugh.

⸺◆⸺

Flynn's team met at a rock face near Lake Taupo. Skies were blue and the sun blared overhead as the group looked up at the climb they were about to undertake. Jenae's neck was all the way cricked backward as she put her sunglasses on to figure out which rocks would make good foot and hand holds.

"Have you ever rock climbed before?" Jenae asked Fiona.

"Nah, but it looks like fun," she replied.

"I don't think I can do this. I have terrible core strength and never thought of myself as a Spiderman character."

"We'll have belay buddies, so they'll keep you from falling to the dirt if your feet slip," Gerry said.

Flynn gathered the group for a briefing by the guide. They learned to put on harnesses, clip in and secure carabiners to a climbing rope.

"Belaying can seem easy but it will require a trust in partners. As the belay, you'll be responsible for each other on the wall. You will stand underneath your climber and watch them at all times. Remember, eyes on your climber at all times. If they fall off of the wall, you are responsible for making sure they descend in a controlled manner and get to the ground safely," the guide instructed.

"All right then, are you ready to find out who your partners are? Remember, this is a trust exercise and I think you will learn that you can trust your life to anyone in this group," Flynn said with a crooked smile.

Jenae crossed her fingers behind her and did a standing backbend as she hoped for Fiona to be her partner.

"First group is Fiona and Gerry." Fiona and Gerry smiled wide and giggled at each other as they scampered off to the rock face.

Flynn read the names and left Jenae until the end.

"And our final group is Jenae and Scottie." Flynn gave Jenae a cheeky glimpse, knowing that Scottie was the person that she trusted the least.

Jenae's head dropped and she pressed her lips together as she watched her life pass before her eyes. *Not Scottie! The one person that irritates me for no reason – other than she's from Scotland and I can't understand a feckin' word she says . . . and that she's four-foot-eight, and pudgy, and has no muscles or strength to hold my weight. What if she yells instructions to me and I can't decipher her accent. I don't even know if her real name is Scottie, that's just what we call her.*

Jenae grimaced as she approached Flynn. "I see what you are doing here, you're getting back at me for last night."

"No, no. I thought you were hilarious last night. No disrespect taken."

"So, are you climbing? Why don't you be my climbing buddy?" Jenae asked.

"I'm just supervising. Scottie needs a climbing partner, and it seems you and her have the most to benefit from this exercise."

"Flynn, you know that she is not strong enough to hold me. What if she loses her grip or gets distracted and I plunge to the ground?"

"You're not giving Scottie enough credit. The ropes are in a pulley system that gives a lot of leeway on strength."

"Alright, but if I die it's all your fault." Jenae kicked rocks as she walked toward Scottie.

Scottie climbed first. Her ascent was slow as expected and Scottie's face matched her flaming red hair when Jenae released her down to the ground with the belay.

"Good job, Scottie," Jenae said.

"I wanted to climb higher, but I don't have much upper body strength and my legs just gave out halfway up," Scottie replied.

"Yeah, you made it about halfway. Are you ready to handle my ropes?"

"Yeah, yeah, sure. Now which way do I hold the cord?" Scottie replied.

Jenae fluttered her eyes closed and said a quick prayer as she pulled on her harness. She called the guide over and asked him to stand next to Scottie. Climbing was as difficult as Jenae had imagined, especially wearing her wide-toed running shoes. Small rocks and dust fell when her foot misplaced and lost a solid grip.

Jenae had a monologue in her head as she climbed, *Three points of contact at all times. Move one limb at a time. Slow and steady gets the work done. Don't look down. Shit, I looked down and Scottie is talking to somebody. She isn't even paying attention to me clinging to this dusty wall.*

"HEY! HEY! Scottie!" Jenae got Scottie's attention. "Have you got me?"

"Oh, yah, I've got you now. I just had a question about the ropes," Scottie hollered back to Jenae.

Flynn walked toward Scottie. "She's got you, Jenae!"

"Hold the rope behind her, would ya? I'm ready to come down." Jenae asked Flynn.

Flynn stood behind Scottie and loosely gripped onto the climbing rope to make sure nothing slipped on Jenae's descent.

The feeling of solid ground under her feet alleviated Jenae's nausea from the climb.

"See, I told you Scottie had you! I didn't have to help at all," Flynn tried his best to candy coat the near disaster.

Fiona handed Jenae a cup of water with a big smile on her face. "That was fun! Gerry and I really clicked – we both made it to the top."

"I'm happy for you. I think I trust Scottie less than I did before. She verified her capabilities to me. I'm glad that's over." Jenae wiped her brow with her sleeve.

<hr>

After a brown bag lunch, the group was rounded up and delivered to the lake's bank with colorful kayaks tied up to random logs littering the beach. Afternoon clouds had moved in, which made the temperature drop enough for everyone to don new lavender windbreakers that had their names embroidered on the chest along with the company's logo. Jenae pulled up her hood and tied the white cord which gave her a turtle look. Two-person and one-person boats were available and Jenae was the first to claim a one-person kayak. A new guide gave instructions on how to put on a life vest, how to enter the water, and how to paddle out to a buoy and back.

Gerry held their boat steady on the water for Fiona as she sunk into the kayak seat. Gerry hopped into the back position as he pushed off shore toward the middle of the lake.

"We are going to win this one!" Fiona shouted back to her coworkers dotting the shore line with her paddle raised to the heavens.

"This isn't a competition!" Flynn yelled back.

Jenae chuckled as Flynn instructed Scotty on how to get into their kayak, and she prayed they would capsize. Her single river kayak had a polyurethane zip up feature that would prevent her from getting soaked. It looked like a wetsuit and zipped like one too.

"Here's the thing with this type of craft. If you capsize, you need to be able to roll back up. Your upper body will get wet, but the boat will stay buoyant."

"How strong does your core need to be? Can I just unzip and escape if I can't get back up?" Jenae asked with concern.

"Sure, as a last resort. We wouldn't want you to drown. But my advice is to go slow and steady so that doesn't happen."

"The wind has really picked up. I won't get stuck out there, will I?" Jenae asked.

"The waves are getting pretty big. Maybe don't go all the way out to the buoy and just stay along the shore line."

Gerry and Fiona headed straight for Jenae as she was getting the hang of paddling and balancing in churning water. They were windblown but their faces beamed and their cheeks were rosy. Fiona lifted her paddle out of the water and splashed Jenae's way.

With an indignant mischievous look, Jenae sang a modified nursery rhyme, "Fiona and Gerry, sitting in a kayak, k-i-s-s-i-n-g. First comes love, then comes marriage, then comes a baby in a baby carriage."

Fiona's face turned bright red and Gerry swiped a formidable splash into Jenae's back.

"Are you engaged yet? Jenae clapped back with a big smile. She wished Neve could be with her to share in the fun.

<hr>

Jenae's late night phone call with Neve helped alleviate some feelings of homesickness. He laughed at her stories and told her that he'd been applying for flying positions while she was away.

"I'll be home the day after tomorrow. Can you pick me up from the airport?" Jenae asked.

"Of course, I'll be there. I miss you," Neve said.

"I can't wait to kiss you. This has been a long week."

"You can tell me all about it when you get home. It's late and I can tell you're bushed," Neve said.

"Yeah, I better get some sleep before tomorrow, we are going on a day-long hike slash obstacle course."

"It sounds like a blast. OK then, goodnight. Love you."

"Nighty night. Love you too."

Birds chirped outside of Fiona's window at the break of dawn, which allowed her to sneak out of the room to meet Gerry for breakfast. Jenae slept in to rest her bones and took a long hot shower to prepare for the last day of challenges.

"Where have you been, missy? Are you just getting in from last night? Were you with Gerry?" Jenae asked.

"Good morning sunshine. As a matter of fact, I was with Gerry . . . for breakfast only. I'm not that kind of girl. I slept here all night. You were dead to the world when I came in. I don't think you moved the entire night," Fiona said.

"Oh, well that's good. You are a sweet girl and I don't want some nerdy guy taking advantage of you." Jenae laughed.

"You think he's a nerd?"

"In a good way. You know, he entertains himself by building boats. He has to have a little geek in him."

"Well, for a nerd, Gerry's a great kisser."

"What? I knew it! You two are going to get married."

"Who knows. You did give him the idea to kiss me after singing that stupid song on the lake."

"Call me cupid and invite me to the wedding!"

"You'll be at the top of the list." Fiona shook her head with a shy smile.

⸻ ◈ ⸻

Flynn reworked the groups to better challenge his reps and to allow them to succeed. He had two levels of the obstacle course and Scottie definitely qualified for the easy one.

Fiona and Jenae were the only females placed on the expert course; the others were all healthy, athletic young men. It started with a bushwhack to the top of a ridge. The marketing manager handled the machete and created a path for others to follow.

"Aren't you glad you brought hiking boots?" Flynn asked the group once they were relaxed and seated at the top of the mountain.

"Fresh air is really nice up here. But, what's the purpose of this obstacle course, Flynn?" Jenae asked.

"Today is about pushing you beyond your limits. I expect all of you to finish the tasks today, but even if you don't, you'll have gone further than you've ever been before."

"Are you a stoic philosopher?" Fiona asked.

"Not completely. But life and work is like a game of millimeters, and to get better at something a little bit at a time is easier than trying to conquer it all at once. We'll be kilometers ahead at the end of a quarter, if each of us improves just one percent. It all adds up," Flynn said.

The marketing manager added, "think about your performance and how you can be one percent better this next quarter."

"Management gave us a dollar amount goal for the end of the fiscal year in July. Our team is on track to meet that goal. We just need a little extra push from all of you," Flynn said.

"What's in it for us?" Gerry asked.

"You'll get a little incentive, but mostly we'll have pride in beating the other teams to the top. It's a challenge. It'll be fun!" Flynn encouraged.

After glissading down a snowy patch from the top of the mountain, the team took turns chopping down a large tree in the forest with a hatchet. Their supplies were limited to what their leaders carried on their backs which added another degree of difficulty.

A final task was to get across a river on a single rope line. Every member had to cross before the group could claim success. The marketing manager led the way by hanging upside down with his ankles crossed like a sloth on a tree limb. The rope was only three inches in diameter and drooped closer to the river as he moved toward the middle.

"Oh crap, it's a good thing we sent the skinny guy first," Flynn shouted.

"I'll re-tie the rope to another tree when I get over," he said as he rhythmically pulled himself – arms then legs until he reached the opposite bank.

Fiona and Jenae were the last over the river, except for Flynn. He was at the back to make sure everyone completed the task. Jenae stopped in the middle for a few moments as she regained her hand strength. She didn't mind the thought of falling in the water below after realizing how difficult it was propelling oneself on a flimsy cord. It reminded her of climbing ropes in middle school gym class. She yelled back to Fiona and Flynn as she dropped to her feet at the end.

"Rope burns are no joke! Make sure your socks are on tight. Dang, that was hard."

Chapter 16

New Year Nuptials

Logan

Boxing Day landed on the start of Logan's last three-day work trip on a fishing vessel in Subic Bay before wedding festivities. He'd gotten down on one knee in front of Joy Lyn's entire family on Christmas Eve and presented her with a size-five marquise shaped diamond ring. It fit perfectly on her left ring finger and her parents beamed with pride when Joy Lyn said, "of course I'll marry you! Yes, yes, yes, a hundred times over. Yes!"

The family had already been planning the festivities after their parish priest had given his blessing. They were just waiting for Logan to pull the trigger. Three o'clock, New Year's Eve was reserved for nuptials in the church.

"Bye! I'll see you at the wedding in a few days?" Logan shouted at his crew as he waved and hauled his duffle bag over his shoulder.

"Sure thing! We wouldn't miss it."

"As long as there's an open bar!"

"And hot chicks!"

"Promise me you'll be on your best behavior at the church," Logan responded to his filthy friends.

On Logan's walk back to his apartment from the docks, a woman screamed and cried hysterically as she pointed to the water below. She spoke Tagalog, but Logan could tell that she had dropped something important in the bay. He stopped and watched as bystanders hurried around. A fisherman jumped into the murky water and popped up with the limp body of her toddler. The mama grabbed her baby girl and cradled and rocked her as she talked and cried. A young airman took the child from her and tried to resuscitate the lifeless body by pounding her back and then breathing into her mouth while pressing on her chest with one hand. Another woman had run into a shop and called for an ambulance.

Logan leaned against a tree and studied the expressions of people helping. The air had a familiar stench of fish and smoke. His heart beat in the sixties as he accidentally smiled at the commotion. Paramedics continued compressions and placed an oxygen mask under the child's chin while they loaded her into the back of the rig. They helped the mother in as well and let her sit at the lower half of the stretcher. Sirens screamed and red and yellow lights flashed as they raced the baby to the hospital.

For twenty minutes, Logan observed and committed to memory facial expressions made by the mom and people around watching and helping. They grimaced and frowned and cried. Their stature changed and they became jittery and some stumbled when they hurried to the scene.

After watching the ambulance disappear down the main road, Logan walked straight to his apartment and went to the bathroom to pee. As he lathered his hands in the sink, he looked at himself in the mirror and tried to imitate the same looks of those empathetic bystanders. He pinched his brows together, frowned, and corded his neck. His eyes watered when he stuck a Q-tip high inside his nose but he could also get a tear-up when he blinked rapidly and looked into the bright lightbulb hanging from the ceiling. He practiced rocking back and forth with his arms crossed and hung his head down. He placed his hands over his face and rubbed his eyes hard enough to get a reddened response. He moaned and cried, "Oh God, No. It can't be!" He shrunk his body and laid his head on his arms that rested on the sink. Logan stood up and took a proud sigh. He pulled down the bottom of his shirt to spread it out and smiled ear to ear in the mirror. "Now that's how you show empathy." Logan clicked his cheek and gave himself two thumbs up.

Joy Lyn and her mother handled all preparations for the New Year's Eve wedding. Auntie prepared flower arrangements and the extended female side of the family cooked an entire weekend to feed an expected one-hundred guests. Ninety-five percent of them were her friends and family, so Joy Lyn wasn't concerned that Logan hadn't contributed much money to the budget. Her best friend's mother was a seamstress and altered Margarita's wedding dress to fit Joy Lyn's tiny waist. It was casual, modest, and sweet like Joy Lyn. Logan had been fitted at the local men's clothing shop for a collarless linen Barong Tagalog shirt. A cream-colored shirt contrasted against dark American style dress pants and matched natural woven loafers.

⸺◆⸻

Guests admired a creche display in a miniature wooden stable that adorned the front of the church as they walked into the main sanctuary for Joy Lyn and Logan's wedding. White ceramic figures were carefully placed looking reverently at the baby Jesus. The baby's hands were raised out of the crib almost touching a lamb, Mary kneeled with perfect prayer hands, Joseph rested his right hand on his heart, an ass and ox laid in protection with a ewe, three wise men held boxes and peered over one another, and a shepherd stood resting a lamb over his shoulders. The shepherd suffered two rock wounds – one in the side of his head and the other gashed his right wrist.

Joy Lyn and her sisters occupied a back room and gazed into a big standing mirror. Margarita helped place a bejeweled comb attached to a veil on top of Joy Lyn's updo. Her best friend popped open a bottle of champagne and poured six glasses of bubbly muscle relaxant into plastic cups.

"Cheers! To my best friend and most beautiful bride ever. You deserve love and especially joy in your life."

Logan had made himself comfortable with his crew buddies outside the back door of the church. They passed around a bottle of whiskey in between jokes and jabs. The priest dressed in all black with a white cardboard collar smiled and waved at the men as he walked from the parsonage to the church.

"I'll see you inside soon, yeah?"

"Five more minutes, Father," Logan said as he waved and gave a thumbs up.

From the back door, the sanctuary looked vast and scary. Pews were full of smiling faces when Logan peeked around the corner of the doorway. His knees buckled and his stomach turned a somersault when the full effect of becoming a husband set in. He hadn't seen Joy Lyn since Christmas, but had talked to her on the phone that morning.

An organist in the balcony abruptly halted a liturgical medley arrangement and began playing "Ava Maria." Groomsmen stepped out to the front of the church, stood in a line and looked back to where Logan waited in a doorway. Bridesmaids walked with perfect measure; each with a small bouquet of flowers held low on their waist. A different groomsman met each of them halfway down the aisle to escort them to their position at the front of the church. Two flower girls diligently tossed flower petals on the aisle while a young ring bearer turned back and waved at the crowd. The best man motioned for Logan to join them as the priest took possession of the rings. Logan walked with his head held high and took deep breaths as he took his place at the front of the altar below the priest.

Joy Lyn peered through a window from the vestibule and smiled when she saw Logan sniffing flowers on his boutonniere. Pepe and Margarita stood by her side at the back entrance of the church. Loud chords from the Wedding March startled guests into standing position as Joy Lyn and her parents calmly walked arm in arm toward the altar. Pepe teared up as he pulled back the veil from her face. Logan shook Pepe's hand and said, "I promise to always take care of your daughter."

Margarita held Pepe's crooked arm and they leaned on each other as they found their spots on the front pew.

Joy Lyn had decided on a quick wedding ceremony without offering the Eucharist since Logan had not yet converted to Catholicism. The entire nuptials lasted thirty minutes, just enough time for readings, prayers, commitment monologues, vows and ring exchange. With his right hand raised, the priest crossed the couple with a body-sized gesture.

"In the name of The Father, and of The Son and of The Holy Spirit."

"Amen."

"I now pronounce you husband and wife. You may now kiss your bride."

Logan looked adoringly at Joy Lyn and gently kissed her tender pink lips.

"Ladies and gentlemen, I present to you Logan and Joy Lyn – man and wife."

The congregation stood and cheered, while Logan picked Joy Lyn up in his arms and carried her down the aisle. Joy Lyn grasped the back of his neck with one hand and raised her bouquet with the other as she was whisked to the exit.

Logan's eyes were wide and filled with tears. "I am the luckiest man in the world!" He laughed and spun Joy Lyn in a circle as if they were already on the dance floor.

<hr>

Big cardboard hats with "1991" glittered on front were handed out to male guests as they entered the reception hall. Women wore cardboard tiaras with "Cheers and Congratulations." The hall was prepared for a New Year's Eve reception. Joy Lyn wore a glittery tiara that took the place of her veil and Logan gently placed his hand at her waist as they were introduced by a DJ standing in the middle of a makeshift dance floor. Logan held Joy Lyn's hands and lifted her left hand and kissed her rings. Joy Lyn looked down and blushed. She had married the man she loved with full consent from her family.

Cold Duck bubbly flowed freely in plastic cups and kept the crowd happy and light headed. Fireworks filled the midnight air, not just from her party but from all around town, and signaled a marital exit on a Jeepney decorated with cans tied on the back. Logan was inebriated but excited to consummate his marriage with his tender bride. Joy Lyn cried as she said her goodbyes to her sisters and parents, especially her father. Logan leaned in and kissed Joy Lyn on the forehead as flashes from cameras blinded the couple.

Chapter 17

First Visitors

Jenae and Neve

News of the marriage of their youngest daughter prompted a well-planned vacation over the new year. Jenae's father splurged for business class tickets because the flight was too long to sit upright in economy all the way to New Zealand. Usually, her parents traveled to far away countries only if a medical conference was part of the package. Jenae's father was a self-confessed workaholic, and wore it as a badge of honor, even though his family viewed it as neglectful at times. He even started an organization called "Xtra-Effort" to validate workaholics worldwide.

Jenae had plenty of time off from her job to show them around. Between four weeks of vacation and royal holidays, she was dumbfounded on how little she worked and wondered how she'd meet her new goals for the company with so much time off. In America, she only had one week of vacation because she never stayed at a job long enough to earn two weeks of vacation. Her parents carved out ten days to spend on the South Island with Jenae and Neve. They stayed the first night at a fancy downtown high-rise hotel to catch up on jet lag before celebrating New Year's Eve. Neve and Jenae arranged dinner at their hotel and invited Helen to join them. Sky high ceilings were adorned with stars and streamers, over white linen covered dining tables. A bottle of champagne sat in the middle of the table that was part of the prix fixe dinner menu. Helen was her usual bubbly self and was happy to have something to do since she was between boyfriends.

❖

Jenae's father paid her back for three tickets booked on the Tranzalpine train from Christchurch to Greymouth. He loved train rides, especially through the beautiful countryside. Neve had a job interview set up for the morning they left, so he dropped the American trio off at the train station on the Main North Line in Addington. He left their luggage in Jenae's company car because he planned to catch up to the train on the West Coast by the time they reached their destination.

The interview went better than Neve expected, and gleefully waited by the car outside the train station. Train views were exquisite, but traveling by car was much quicker. He saw Jenae seated in the third car with her face pressed up against a large viewing window. He waved to her and her mom pointing his way. Steam flooded out of the top of the engine and steel wheels whined to a stop.

"How was the train ride?" Neve asked.

"It was fabulous! One of the best rides I've ever taken. Thanks for bringing the car over, Neve," Dad said.

"How was the drive? How long have you been waiting for us?" Jenae asked.

"Just a few minutes. I must confess that I saw the train go over the ridge and I raced down to beat you."

"Let's go! Neve is going to show us around his old cop beat before we head south," Jenae said.

"Greymouth is a small town, so it won't take too long."

The foursome drove straight to Queenstown and made it to their hotel rooms just in time to shower and get ready for their dinner reservation at a highly rated restaurant nearby. Their boutique hotel sat on the edge of Lake Wakatipu and the walk to the eatery was cooler than Jenae had expected. Jenae took a deep breath through her nose and said, "Ahh. I haven't smelled pine trees since I left America."

"I'll have a rack of lamb. I had to have lamb while here and I read that the chef is divine. It should have been noted on our reservation," Dad told the waitress.

"Yes sir, it certainly was. You were smart to let us know ahead of time because we do run out of lamb every night. The chef will have your orders out soon."

Mom ordered a Manhattan cocktail and the rest had a local beer on tap.

"A toast to our very first visitors from America!" Clinks in the middle of the table caught the attention of a bored couple seated at the window. They were "that" couple who'd had enough vacation time together and nothing left to discuss.

"I have an announcement to make." Neve raised his eyebrows and widened his eyes.

"What's that, Neve?" Mom asked.

"My interview went well this morning and the airline has offered me a tentative offer to fly commuter routes in Tahiti!"

"Oh, how wonderful! Cheers to Neve getting his first real flying job!" Mom said as they clinked their glasses again. The bored couple joined in and gave congratulations.

"We need to talk about your job offer," Jenae said.

"What's there to talk about? I got a great offer from Air Tahiti. Sure, it's a French airliner, but I only have to go away for two weeks in a row and then I'm back home for three weeks."

"You're going to leave me here for two weeks at a time? You realize that I have exactly one friend here in New Zealand. Fiona is going to get sick of me," Jenae said.

"But you can come and stay with me in Tahiti while I fly the commuter routes. Who doesn't want to spend time in Tahiti?"

"Neve! I have a job here. Am I supposed to quit?"

"I guess we can't afford that. I'll just try it out for a few months and see how it goes. Maybe I'll find a better job by the time you run out of vacation days. It's only about a three-hour flight from here."

Jenae rolled over in bed away from Neve and tried to fall asleep.

The next morning came quickly with a jet boat ride on the lake. Mom had suggested the ride because she always had a need for speed. A bloke with reflective sporty sunglasses helped all six passengers into his red boat after helping secure their life jackets.

"Who wants to go fast?" the driver said.

"This lady right here." Jenae pointed to her mom who looked like a babushka with a large head scarf tied under her chin.

"Alrighty then, hold on to your hats. Here we go!"

Jenae and Neve were slammed into their seats in the back of the boat as it sprinted into the middle of the lake. It reminded Jenae of boat racing off the coast of Florida, where the hull barely made contact with the water's surface.

"Wah!" Mom screamed with glee as the boat turned side to side.

"We're going to head to the cliff over there and slow down to navigate some cave structures."

Dad was relieved to hear the words, "slow down." Even Mom was a little bit relieved because a mist blowing against her face felt like ice pellets at a high speed.

"That was refreshing!" Jenae said as they wobbled down the dock.

—◆◇◆—

A gondola ride to the top of a mountain for lunch gave the foursome an aerial view of the longest lake on the South Island. Their window table gave Neve the sensation of approaching an airport for landing.

"So, tell us more about your job at Tahiti Air," Jenae said.

"It'll be a great opportunity for me to get experience and rack up a bunch of flight hours. It should get me to the major airlines fairly quickly," Neve said.

"Jenae told us that you'll be gone for a couple weeks at a time," Dad commented.

"Yeah, but I hope she can come visit me during that time. It would be a great vacation for her. You two can come visit also. Have you ever been to Tahiti?" Neve asked.

"Oh no, we haven't, that would be fabulous! I would love that! Did you know that Jenae's brother was in a stage play, South Pacific, when he was a boy? The story is based in Tahiti," Mom said to Neve.

"Yeah, I think she told me about that. What song did he sing?"

"Dite-moi, Pour quoi?" Mom started to sing. "Tell me why."

"You'll need to learn French. I'll teach you what I learned in high school and college," Jenae said.

"Lucky for me, air traffic control is always in English," Neve said.

"You can start with, *Parlez-vous, Anglais?*"

On the drive to Franz Joseph and Fox glaciers, Mom saw helicopters with tourist lettering flying overhead.

"Who wants to go on a helicopter ride with me? Mom said.

"Not me," Jenae said.

"Not me," Dad said.

"I'll stay behind and hike to the glacier instead," Neve said.

Mom found her way to a van with similar advertising in the parking lot as they pulled in.

"Let me off here, I'm going to check if they have availability."

Neve pulled into a parking spot nearest the glacier and sprinted back to check on Mom.

"They've got a spot for me in fifteen minutes. We're going to land on the glacier up top and have a look around."

"We'll hike to the glacier lake while you are airborne. Come find us when you land."

"They said the trip lasts thirty minutes."

Neve hurried to Jenae and Dad as they were in deep conversation walking to the face of a glacier. Cosmic blue colors glistened from a mineral based ice wall. A waterfall flowed down to a small body of water below.

"Your mom has inspired me. I'm going to stand underneath that waterfall. Here, take my picture." Neve handed Jenae his camera as he undressed down to his shorts and trainers.

"Get all the way under! I want to see the water hitting your face!" Jenae hollered in his direction.

Neve stood proudly under the direct flow of freezing water plunging from fifty feet above. His arms were outstretched as he endured the painful pelting of the ultimate cold shower.

"Ouch, ow! Damn, that was cold. It felt like ice shards falling down on my face."

"Are you OK? That was a lot of energy falling on your head. Your eye looks red," Dad said.

"It was a lot worse than I imagined it would be. Knock that off my bucket list." Neve shivered and put his pants, shirt and jacket back on.

Jenae hugged him to give him body heat. "You're my brave husband."

<hr>

The day before Jenae's parents returned to the States, Neve's father, Peter, made lunch reservations at a fancy rustic restaurant for the group. Neve was surprised that he had made such an effort, because he only knew the penny-wise stingy father as a young child. Jenae's dad showed appreciation for Peter's treat and engaged in meaningful conversation. He was good at making others feel at ease, even though he was a foreigner in their country.

"You remind me of a general," Peter complimented Jenae's dad. "I mean, you look like one from a great war with your beard and large stature."

"Maybe I'm channeling a great-great grandfather, General Desaix. He fought with Napoleon. My middle name is Desaix.

"He can be savage and diplomatic at the same time. Two of my favorite traits," Jenae said.

"I don't think we have any generals on our side of the family, but I did join a submarine crew at age fourteen for World War II. It was the ultimate adventure, and my parents were certain I'd die in a metal can at the bottom of the ocean," Peter said.

"I couldn't join the military because I was a blue baby. That was the term back then. I've got a heart murmur," Dad said. "My father was a Marine and told me stories about training the troops in bayonet hand-to-hand combat. I'm sure he was disappointed that I couldn't follow in his footsteps – I went to medical school instead."

Neve was surprised and relieved that the patriarchs had enjoyed each other's company. He saw Peter through a more favorable lens.

Chapter 18

Tahiti Hops

Jenae and Neve

Two barefoot men in red wrap skirts, and straw hats, swayed side to side playing ukuleles alongside a hula dancer, as Neve stood in line for customs. A sign above a wood and stone stage read, "Manava – Bienvenue a Tahiti." They sang a high energy tune in a language he didn't understand, but knew it wasn't French. A beautiful woman on stage wore a brown and white tropical patterned top and long skirt, with her mid-section showing, and a big white flower on the side of her head. She was calm and serene as she moved her arms fluidly. She touched her mouth with her left hand and swooped her arms, as if gathering the world, then brought them back to her body for a hug as she swayed her hips back and forth.

"Ah, that's better. I didn't have time to use the bathroom on the plane before we landed," Jenae looked around and grabbed her passport. How fun!"

"I'm glad you came with me to visit for my first weekend. You can come back and jump seat on my flights and island hop with me. I'm sure there'll be extra seats."

"I could get used to this lifestyle. Maybe I can pack five days of work into three or four and hang out in Tahiti with you." Jenae's eyes lit up when they passed a pearl jewelry store after passing through customs. A man with a personalized sign helped load their suitcases into the boot of a sedan and greeted them in English.

"Welcome to Pape'ete. Have you been here before?"

"This is our first visit. I'm starting a job here."

"Oh yeah? What do you do?"

"I'm a pilot." The words that came out of Neve's mouth felt real for the first time. He'd dreamed of saying them for what seemed like forever, and he couldn't believe that he made it.

"It looks like the airline put you up at the nicest hotel on the island. They must be really happy that you will be flying for them." The driver swerved on a roundabout to miss a chicken crossing the road.

"I'm really happy that they hired me. Je suis extatique!" Neve said.

"Trés bien, parlez-vous français?"

"Un peu, mais j'apprends," Neve knew a little more than he let on.

"Bien."

"When did you learn that? I guess I haven't been paying enough attention," Jenae said.

"The company sent me a book and tapes to learn. I've been listening on my runs."

"A bientôt!"

Neve checked in at the front desk and had arranged for a special occasion reception in their room. Jenae sipped a cup of citrus water and waited in an open-air reception area while Neve got the keys. A bellman loaded their luggage and told them that he'd meet them at their bungalow. "Take your time, enjoy the property. There's lots to see." Slow paced Island time was an adjustment and an annoyance for Jenae.

Barbecued pork aroma wafted from the side of a restaurant. Visitors laid out by a pool just meters from a lagoon and a freshwater pond with native fish and birds. The roped sidewalk led them to the bungalow area along the shoreline.

"Here we are!" Neve opened the door with his key and motioned for Jenae to enter first.

"Did you get us a bungalow?" Jenae hopped and skipped through the small hallway to an overwater bedroom lagoon suite.

"The company reserved it for us for just one night, and we'll move to a regular room for the rest of the time," Neve said.

"Oh my God! Look at all of the flower arrangements in the room. Look at the bed! The towels look like two swans kissing. There are one, two, three, four, five flower arrangements on the bed. Sit down, I want to take a picture with them. Careful, don't blow the petals off."

"Do you like it?"

"Of course, I love it. Look at that amazing arrangement on the coffee table and over there – on the sleeper sofa. There's even a bird-of-paradise in the champagne cooler," Jenae said.

"Let's pop that open and celebrate on the deck. We're just in time for sunset." Neve poured champagne into glasses and set them on top of another flower arrangement on the patio table. Jenae sat in his lap and kissed his lips in between bubbly sips.

"I'm so proud of you for reaching your dream. You're a real commercial pilot! You are getting paid for what you love, can you believe it?" Jenae said.

"I feel like the luckiest man in the world. You coming into my life has brought me good fortune, Jenae."

"I love you so much."

It may have been a long travel day, too much champagne, an extended sex session, or maybe the effect of sleeping above negative ions in the overwater bungalow, but Jenae passed out and missed dinner altogether.

A fish nursery flourished below their above water room in a reef below. Jenae sat on the deck and watched baby fish skirt around coral looking for breakfast once the sun rose. Neve curled up in the sheets and slept off the night before.

Neve found Jenae with her feet gently swishing the water's surface from a deck below. She had mixed feelings about Neve living and working away from her for two weeks at a time. He couldn't pass up the opportunity, but she couldn't join him, nor could they afford to live there as a couple. The cost of living was too high, especially on his meager starting salary.

The company set Neve up at a crash pad with other pilots, but it wasn't a place Jenae could visit on a regular basis.

"Hey sleepyhead. Are you hungry for breakfast?" Jenae asked.

"Let's go to the buffet, I think they are still serving."

Morning fog clouds moved in during a walking tour around the property. Neve stopped to pick fresh flowers off a tree along the way.

"I don't suppose you need any more flowers, but here is a fresh one for your hair."

"That's sweet." Jenae smelled its honey fragrance and placed it behind her ear. Neve adjusted the petals and kissed her cheek.

"Are you going to be OK with me gone? I'll have two weeks on and three weeks off. So you'll get sick of me when I'm home, I'm sure," Neve said.

"It'll be fine, really." Jenae looked down and felt soreness in her throat and heaviness in her arms.

"I'm doing this for us. It won't be forever, I promise."

"I know, but I'll miss you. You know Fiona is my only friend in Christchurch."

"You say that, but you make friends so easily. It's your super-talent."

"Aw, thanks." Jenae tried to smile at Neve's contrived compliment.

"Let's go snorkeling! I want you to take a picture of me under the bungalow, through the glass coffee table. It'll be cool."

"OK, show off."

<hr>

Helen picked Jenae up on the front curb of Christchurch airport. She was a skilled stick shift driver and rolled every stop sign along the way.

"How fabulous is this opportunity for Neve, and you," Helen said.

"Yeah, I'm going to miss him, but I can immerse myself in work and go to the gym more while he's away," Jenae said. Her only other major activities included watching weekend long cricket matches on tele and riding her bike on two lane country roads.

"How would you like to go for a car ride in the countryside with me next weekend? I can show you around parts that you don't see on your work route."

"Sure, that'd be great!"

"We could go to a movie sometime, too." Helen raised her eyebrows and cocked her head. "Oh, by the way, a big envelope arrived for you at my house. It's from America. I've had it for a week, so I hope it isn't important" Helen said as she dug around the back seat of her car.

"I'll get it when we stop. Don't crash for me."

Helen pulled up to the front of Jenae's tall condo building. She wasn't used to going into the front door and certainly not used to occupying the apartment all by herself. Her stomach fluttered as she unloaded her bags from the back seat.

"Don't forget your post!" Helen pointed to a large manila envelope stuck under the passenger seat.

"Got it. Thanks for picking me up. I'll give you a call later to figure out next weekend."

"Oh, there's another letter for you from the Philippines." Helen pulled down her sun visor and slipped out the envelope. She leaned out of the passenger window and handed it to Jenae.

"Who do I know in the Philippines?" Jenae waved at Helen before she rolled another stop sign and peeled out of the parking lot.

A bowl of cereal filled up Jenae's belly for dinner. She was too tired to cook and had found a knock off Cheerios brand on her last visit to the grocery store. She poured cow's milk sparingly and covered the top with a generous tablespoon of sugar sprinkle. She thought about refilling the bowl with more cereal after finishing one serving, but didn't like ultra-sweet milk at the bottom of the bowl. Jenae gagged when she thought about her brothers who drank sugary milk from the bottom of the bowl.

The battered brown manila envelope from Helen caught her attention; she recognized her ex-roommate's handwriting, and hoped it wasn't filled with bills from San Francisco. Four letters fell out onto the kitchen table from the pouch. They were initially postmarked eight and nine months prior and all had the same handwriting in blue pen.

Hm, these must have come right after I moved out. I guess it was sent on a slow boat through China.

Logan had written manifesto style letters, four and five pages long. Jenae leaned back in her chair frozen with her eyes bulging. *He isn't dead!*

Chapter 19

Mink and Mini Mink

Logan

Ten months flew by, especially when reinventing oneself as a fisherman from Australia and saying "I do." Joy Lyn was a perfect bride and wife. Logan felt a tinge of guilt when he took her virginity on their wedding night. Once the initial shock of first time vaginal penetration wore off, Joy Lyn became every man's fantasy – a freak in the sheets. Logan had never had better sex probably because he truly loved her.

Joy Lyn continued to work for families on the American Air Force base while Logan fished and worked as a deckhand for days at a time on the water. Volunteering at the Catholic orphanage kept her busy after church on Sundays, which always seemed to be a workday for Logan. After church and family dinner, Joy Lyn spent a few hours consulting mothers with unwanted pregnancies who usually visited in their third trimester. She also loved spending time rocking babies in the nursery. She was hopeful that Logan would impregnate her sooner than later. She was anxious to start her own family and planned to have at least four children.

⊷◈⊷

"Hey Logan, a young lady was wandering around the docks this week asking if anyone knew you." Logan's old neighbor stopped him while he cleaned fish guts off his rubber boots and fishing pants. Joy Lyn didn't like the nastiness of the sea brought into their love cottage. Their abode wasn't big, but she kept it clean and filled it with love.

"Oh yeah? Who was that? Was she cute?"

"I suppose she was alluring in a pole dancer kind of way."

"Oh crap, I hope she isn't coming after me for money."

"Maybe, maybe not. She had a baby with her."

Logan stopped, put down the hose and looked up.

"A baby huh. What did she say?" Logan stuttered.

"She said she met you when you first moved to the Philippines. She was your girlfriend."

"My girlfriend? Did she tell you her name?" Logan asked.

"Yeah, it was something, Mink. She called the baby Mini Mink."

"Oh shit, yeah I remember her."

"She left a note, let me grab it for you."

Logan read words scratched on the back of a napkin and carefully counted the months that had passed on all ten of his fingers.

"She says the baby's mine. This could be anybody's baby – she worked at the Eager Beaver. She was never my girlfriend. Well, maybe I paid for a week of her time, but that was it."

"You can't tell Joy Lyn. If her father finds out you have a child out of wedlock, he'll beat the hell out of you."

"It can't be my baby."

"There's no way to tell, but she kind of had your forehead and your eyes."

"Shit man. I'll get in touch with her this week. If she comes around again, tell her I left town."

"There's a law in the Philippines against adultery, you know. They'll throw you in jail if there's evidence of it. Like a living child."

Logan stopped into a local bar and took two shots of vodka before he caught the bus home.

<hr>

June Mink breastfed six-week-old Mini Mink on the public bus, after leaving the docks. The bouncing motion kept baby Mink from fussing. A polite young man at the back of the bus stood up to offer her his seat. She wiped tears rolling down her face with the baby's extra corner of a receiving blanket that the hospital let her take home. They also gave her a bag with cloth diapers, disposable wipes, a set of onesies, and baby socks. Mini Mink's belly button was completely healed and her full head of black hair had little skin scabs stuck on her scalp under a knit cap. A nurse from the hospital checked on June and MM a couple of times at her parent's home. She assured June that MM was healthy except for a minor case of cradle cap that was easily remedied by brushing the baby's hair or gently scratching it with clean fingers. The nurse included a referral form in the bag to the Catholic orphanage which was walking distance from the next bus stop.

June had sobbed when her dad threw her and MM out of the house. He was disgusted, and greedy for June's earnings from local bars.

"How could you get pregnant and not tell us?" her mom said.

"Now we are stuck with your bastard child! You need to get back to work at the Eager Beaver."

"I love her. She is mine."

"We can't afford to feed her. You need to find the father or give her away." Her father walked out of the house and lit a cigarette.

June was mostly sure MM was Logan's child, but had little hope that she'd find him. And even if she did, he'd likely deny paternity if he was smart. The same young man that gave up his seat picked up her bags and helped June down the bus steps.

Diesel exhaust puffed at her feet. "Thank you, for being so kind." June had a new appreciation for thoughtful men, and in a moment of desperation she wondered if the teenager was old enough to marry her and take care of her forever. She snapped out of her delusion and made her way on a path back to a large metal gate at the front of the orphanage property. A guard sitting in a tiny booth popped his head out of the window when she approached.

"Can I help you lady?"

"I need to talk to somebody about my baby."

"Yes ma'am. Let me call a nun to come out. Here, come inside the gate and have a seat."

June Mink sat on a park bench situated under a large shade tree while she waited.

"Do you want a cup of water? I just came on duty; I have a fresh jug." He pointed to a large orange thermos.

"Thank you. Sure, if you don't mind."

———◆———

Sister walked with June down a long dirt path to the orphanage hidden in a jungle canopy.

"Your baby's beautiful. Do you want me to carry her for you?"

"Yes please, thank you. She's a really good baby. Her name is Mini Mink. MM for short."

June felt safe in the facility and observed children happy and plump in the arms of nuns and volunteers caring for them. She explained to the head sister that she didn't have any support from her family or the father. She admitted that she was a bar girl and had made a mistake, although MM was not a mistake to her.

The nun who walked her in suggested that June take her time in deciding the fate of MM. A head nun handed her an envelope with money to spend a few nights at a local motel nearby.

"Please pray for discernment about baby Mini Mink. She is a child of God, and we will prepare a crib and care for her if you decide that for her. I'm sure we could find a loving family for her. This is a momentous decision," Sister said.

"Thank you. I only want the best for her, and I might not be able to provide the life she deserves."

"God will provide. Come back in a few days if you wish to put her up for adoption."

⸺◆⸺

Logan made his way back to Joy Lyn just in time for dinner and offered to set and clear the table. He dried dishes and put them away in the cupboard before handing Joy Lyn a bottle of lotion.

"Come sit on the couch with me, honey. I'll rub your feet. You've been working too hard." Logan kissed her on the back of her neck.

"What are you up to? Why are you being so nice to me?"

"I've been thinking, we need to try harder to get you that baby you want so badly."

Joy Lyn laid down on the sofa and propped her feet up on Logan's lap. She fidgeted her toes around his crotch and tucked one underneath. He closed his eyes as tension built in his swollen pants.

Joy Lyn laughed. "You're just horny. Let's see how well you can rub my feet. I may let you go all the way to the top of my legs."

Logan had mixed feelings about her unshaven legs. It was sexy, but weird, like he was with a guy. Her hairy armpits were his biggest hurdle in getting an erection. As long as she kept a shirt on or was on all fours he could keep his little titi up. He usually thought about Jenae's soft skin and sweet smile when he ejaculated into Joy Lyn's womb. *I've really got to take her to a spa to get her waxed. I wonder if they do nipples too.*

Chapter 20

Truth and Consequences

Jenae - Logan

Jenae blinked her eyes awake, and pulled crusties off of a few lashes that didn't want to unstick. Light from a floor lamp next to the living room couch disappeared into the rays of sun that glowed in from picture windows. The velvet sectional couch wasn't as comfortable as she thought it would be. She stretched her back and pressed the palms of her hands against her forehead to make sense of the letters she'd read the night before.

But she couldn't. She'd imagined for the past year that she'd left the dangers of Logan behind in the cold choppy waters of San Francisco Bay.

He jumped! He had to have jumped.

Jenae had no fear until the letters showed up in her mother-in-law's post box. Her stalker was alive and well and knew where she lived, or at least where Neve used to live.

She'd read books on psychopaths who had troubled upbringings caused by physical and mental abuse. And many had their brains altered at birth from mothers who drank or did drugs during pregnancy. Some were damaged by an overly doting mother who turned her son into a golden boy. Just one damaged lobe of their brain could determine if he, (usually a male) would turn into a pathological menace to society. She could call Logan a monster, but that would be too harsh even for Jenae.

The letter from the Philippines scared her the most. Logan claimed that he had learned to control his impulsivity and had built a life up from nothing. His Mea Culpa included assurances that all grievances against Neve were cleared up before he left the States. He had made sure that Neve's record was clean from his false accusations, and if he ever wanted to return to America and apply for a green card or citizenship in the future, he should be fine.

After putting on her running shoes and track pants, Jenae hopped in the elevator. Hagley Park was beckoning her to breathe in its cool piney air. She looked at her watch and moved the outer dial to match the minute hand. It was 8:20 AM.

She hadn't discounted any threat that could be inferred by Logan knowing their location and was tempted to call Neve to tell him the good and the bad news. But she didn't want to do anything to worry Neve on his first week of training because she knew he would focus on the bad stuff.

Neve would have his uniform soon with bars on his shoulders. *I wonder if they wear tropical shirts at the Tahitian*

Airline, or do they look more buttoned up and professional like the bigger airlines?

⸻ ◆ ⸻

Jenae led Fiona by the wrist into a cafe where people were waiting in line to order pots of tea and scones at the counter.

"Thanks for meeting me for afternoon tea."

"No worries."

Fiona ordered first and Jenae paid for both orders – technically the company paid because tea was reimbursed twice a day on weekdays.

"Am I in trouble?" Fiona asked.

"That depends," Jenae said. "Is something going on with Gerry that you haven't told me about?"

"Why would you think something is going on?"

"Because he called me to ask what you liked to eat. Did he come visit you while I was gone?"

"You caught me."

"Fiona! How could you keep this from me?"

"I didn't want to jump the gun," Fiona said.

"You are my best friend, but I don't mind sharing you with Gerry," Jenae said.

"Aw, I'm your best friend?"

"Well, honestly you're my only friend here, so don't be too flattered."

"OK then, as long as we are besties – Gerry and I are kissing and stuff. I guess we're boyfriend and girlfriend now."

"That's so exciting! I'm happy for both of you."

"So how was Tahiti? I'm so jealous, I've never been."

"Maybe you and Gerry can go there on your honeymoon. At most, it's a four-hour flight."

"There you go jumping the gun again."

Jenae poured another cup of tea and looked panicked. She told her only friend in New Zealand about her still alive stalker.

"I don't know if I can deal with him again. He might come here and screw with Neve and me."

"Just calm down. He's not coming to New Zealand. Even if he did, you have all of us to take care of you."

"He's got a wife and family in the Philippines now. Surely, he wouldn't mess that up."

"Holy shit, how did he find a wife already?"

"I know, it doesn't add up."

⸺◆⸺

Breathe, in two, three, four. Hold two, three, four, five, six, seven. Out, two, three, four, five, six, seven, eight. I don't feel more relaxed, my head is going to explode, Logan thought.

That was the ritual the FBI taught to activate his parasympathetic system when he was in stressful situations.

"Release all thoughts," they'd told him. But his chest returned to shallow ins and outs after he talked to June Mink on the phone. His ex-neighbor had broken down and gave her his new phone number when she returned looking for him.

He agreed to meet her at his cottage with baby Mini Mink. Joy Lyn would be none the wiser while she worked at her job on base and wouldn't be home until dinnertime.

It was a long shot, but all June Mink had was long shots to find the baby's real daddy. She had it narrowed down to two white men because MM looked more Caucasian then Filipino. The other man in the running had moved back to the U.S.

"I'm just doing some math in my mind." Logan rubbed his head and pulled on the fine hairs left on top of his head.

"She looks just like you, Mahal."

"I'm not Mahal, who the hell is Mahal. Is he the daddy?"

"No Logan, it's the nickname I gave you when we were making love. It means, 'my love.'"

"It's been a long time since you stole my money and ran off."

"About ten and a half months. That's how I know Mini Mink is your child."

"I don't believe it. You're just trying to shake me down for more money."

"I love you, I swear. I've always loved you. I just wanted to get out of the business so I had to run far from my father. He wouldn't let me quit."

She saw him looking at MM. "Her eyes do look familiar."

"See, see? She looks exactly like you."

"You knew this the whole time you were pregnant? Why didn't you try to find me earlier? I mean, shit!"

He looked at her and baby MM. His face twisted with lips pursed.

"You've got to get out of here with this baby. Right now! I'm married!" His emotion of fear had turned to rage as he replayed a conversation he'd had about adultery and children out of wedlock. His father's crazy brother promised Logan that if he mis-stepped in the marriage with his niece, his days would be numbered.

Logan didn't care if either of them lived or died. He stared down at his hands and imagined them around June's throat. She had seen that look before, from her father.

His screaming and black eyes scared June to hurriedly slide MM into a banana sling around her body. She covered the baby's head with her forearm as she packed up a diaper bag and scurried out of the front door.

He would prefer her purged from the world – to save his future. Logan wanted her to look back at him as she walked down the path, to scare her enough that she would know not to come back. She didn't.

Chapter 21

Train Game

Jenae

In some ways, the train tracks could have been located in Anywhere, Kansas. Wind swept long grass, a barn, and a little hotel seemed straight out of a show from the sixties. The only part missing was three wholesome girls from Petticoat Junction pulling sundresses off a water tower.

Dark fumes billowed from a smoke stack and came around the corner with a train's whistle leading the way. An engineer leaned out of his cab and waved his blue and white cap at a group of overprivileged pharmaceutical reps standing on a once well-used wooden platform. They jumped back behind a red line as the engine, piled up with chopped wood, slowed down with steam that forcefully spewed from both sides.

"Everybody, load up!" Flynn motioned to his minions.

"Where are we going?"

"It's a surprise, as usual. You'll know when we get there." Flynn had a fetish for big reveals.

Three people on a dirt road waved to the two-car train as it leisurely chugged down its tracks and stopped short of the only general store around. A young lady with a basket of apples waved them down and passed the fruit on to the engineer with a wink and blown kiss. Who in turn, handed them to a wrinkle-faced man with a black hat. It was a multigenerational operation.

"Would you like a crisp Fuji apple?" he asked all twelve passengers. "They were picked right over there at my son's orchard. We are one of the oldest orchards on the North Island."

"This reminds me of the Sugar Cane Train in Maui. It moved sugar cane in the old days, but now it's a tourist attraction," Jenae said to Fiona and Gerry seated in front of her.

"You've been everywhere!" Fiona looked back at Jenae and Flynn.

"Well anyway, Maui is fantastic for a honeymoon. What do you think, Gerry?"

Fiona's face turned red and she turned to look out the window.

"I get it," Flynn said. "I've been to America. The country is huge and people are willing to travel a long way to get somewhere."

"That's why he hired me, you know. Because he has an obsession with America." Jenae waved her thumb at Flynn.

"I'm just hoping Jenae and Neve will put me up there someday. I know you'll go back," Flynn said.

Peanut shells littered the hardwood planks under tables at the bar. The company's budget for this quarterly retreat was tight, to make up for past lavish events. Platters of fish and chips and shepherd's pie were placed in the middle of a large, carved wooden table big enough for the dozen divas.

"Did you bring us to a bar for dinner, Flynn?" Jenae asked.

"Ah, the train ride bunged up my budget. It was between this and an expensive hoity-toity restaurant in town that didn't have enough seating for all of us. Good news is we have an unlimited budget for beer," Flynn said.

Jenae thought back to her undergraduate college days, which included drinking games after midterms and finals. Her sorority sisters often filled a large booth, and pitchers of beer were delivered to their table until happy hour ended. Music on the jukebox usually included hits by John Cougar Mellencamp and REO Speedwagon. Off-tune crooning got louder and more obnoxious as their favorite game Quarters made a few rounds about the table.

"Can I have a pitcher of light beer, please?" Jenae asked the Kiwi waitress.

"We have diet beer. Is that what you mean?

"Sure, I guess so. You don't have a light beer?"

"No, sorry."

"I'm going to the bathroom. When I get back, I'm going to show all of you how to play quarters," Jenae teased the reps.

One doorway led to another door jamb, which led to a crooked bathroom marked for women. It was actually more than one room. She turned the handle and pushed, but felt resistance and heard a shearing sound each time she gave a little shove to open it.

"Hello? Is anybody in there?"

The door finally opened after Jenae gave it a final thrust with her right shoulder leading the charge.

The empty room was decorated with plastic flowers and doilies on an antique dresser next to a rusty toilet. There was another room leading off of it, separated by a thick curtain. She peeked around the dark blue curtain to make sure no creepers were hanging out to watch her use the loo.

Jenae used thin squares of paper from a silver dispenser to wipe her bottom. They tore apart. No paper towels or soap meant she had wet patches on her thighs after rinsing her hands in the sink.

"OK, who knows how to play Quarters?" Jenae asked.

Her coworkers looked dismayed at her inquiry.

"OK, maybe it's called a twenty-cent piece here. Or maybe fifty-cent pieces?" Jenae pulled coins out from her wallet and threw them in the middle of the table. Even the slightly shy and most awkward coworkers perked up.

Flynn was thrilled to add fun and flair to their work excursion.

"You may get a little tipsy with this game."

To her chagrin, nobody spoke up, but they looked amused when she explained the rules.

"So, what you are saying is . . . we each have a glass of beer, and we toss a coin off of the table into somebody's glass that we target to chug the whole thing?" Gerry asked.

"Exactly, so if you want Flynn to drink, try to bounce it into his cup," Jenae said.

Fifty-cent coins didn't bounce high enough, so they switched to twenty-cent pieces. Flynn was targeted, but three glasses of beer didn't faze his sobriety. Jenae tasted diet beer for her first chug and found it light but bitter. Her taste buds resisted and she smacked her lips with a grimace and twisted face after it hit her stomach.

"Well, that is the worst light beer I've ever tasted!"

"Alright then team. You heard her. It's the worst beer she's tasted!"

After four more chugs in a row, Jenae turned pale and stood up with the assistance of both hands on the table. The table chuckled as they watched her hold onto wallpapered walls on her journey back to the women's toilet. She yakked the same five beers into a rusty toilet. Color and taste hadn't changed much from when she'd gulped them down.

Fiona rushed into the open door to the bathroom. All she could see was Jenae's backside in a pike position leaned over the toilet bowl.

"Are you OK? Here, let me hold your hair." Fiona grabbed tissues and put her arm around Jenae's back.

"Are you done? Do you want to wash your mouth out at the sink?"

Fiona combed her hair and put Jenae back together again for appearances. A walk of shame back to the table was worth purging a six pack of poison from her stomach.

The train had retired to its station for the night – to rest up for the next tourist excursion. A tattered old school bus picked them up at the bar to drive them to their hotel. Jenae had no interest in singing along with the others to "99 bottles of beer." Bitter notes of diet beer remained on her tongue.

"Does anyone have a Tic Tac?"

⬤

The South Islanders waited in the club room at Wellington airport for their flights home the next day. They rehydrated with tea, coffee and sodas. Flynn hung out with them to debrief his crew.

"Well, that was fun last night. Good innocent fun and lots of bonding. We learned new things from each other and some took care of each other in their time of need. I hope everyone is feeling well enough to travel without a sick sack in their lap.

Now let's finish out the fiscal year with a big number in sales. We're almost there and I think we'll have awards to pass out next retreat if we reach our goals. And next time, you South Islanders won't have to travel on an airplane to get there. We are coming to you! We are going snow skiing!"

Fiona hugged Gerry goodbye and he took her around a corner to give her a peck on the lips. Fiona felt pain and pleasure in their long-distance relationship that was complicated by a no-nepotism rule in the company. Gerry was willing to relocate to the South Island and find another job for her.

Diet beer remained etched in her memory forever, but the hangover from the weekend was erased when Jenae thought about seeing her husband again. Neve would be home from two weeks away at his new job. She couldn't wait to hear about flying in the beautiful tropics and dreaded revealing letters they'd received from Logan.

Chapter 22

Family Life

Logan

June Mink stood outside the gates of the orphanage. It took her thirty-seconds to decide to put Mini Mink up for adoption and a twenty-minute bus ride to reach the stop. Logan's threatening response scared her more than her father's threats. Mini Mink deserved a better chance at survival than anyone in her life could give her.

"We can take her today once you've filled out all of the paperwork." A sister pointed to a package containing a stack of papers.

"Do I have to put down the father's name?" June asked.

"Only if you know for sure. Have you talked to the father?"

"I just left him. He doesn't want anything to do with me or the baby."

June wrote down Logan's name. At least the name she knew him by when he arrived last summer. She breastfed MM one more time and changed her diaper.

"You can call and check on her once a week. And we'll contact you when she gets adopted."

June Mink nodded her head as she held Mini Mink next to her face.

"I love you sweet girl. I'm sorry I have to leave you, but I know you will have a better life without me in it right now."

MM fell asleep in her arms and June wiped away tears from her eyes.

"Let's say a prayer before you leave," Sister said.

"OK." June crossed herself.

"Heavenly Father, we give thanks for the life of Mini Mink and that you have blessed the earth with her presence. We pray for her safety and future life with a loving family. We pray for continued protection of June and give her peace of mind in her discernment. In Jesus' name we pray. AMEN."

"AMEN." June crossed herself again.

⚬

Five and a half months of marriage without getting pregnant surprised her. June Lyn thought she would have conceived a child with Logan by then, and worried that she may be infertile. How could she live the life she'd planned for in childhood, while playing with baby dolls – without a real child of her own?

She volunteered at the orphanage every Sunday evening when Logan was working on a fishing rig, which was more frequent than either had counted on. He seemed more distant, and happy to take on extra shifts for money. Logan assured her that it was to raise capital for his own fishing boat one day. And hard work had sapped him of energy. Energy that he didn't have for intimacy with Joy Lyn.

Rocking babies filled Joy Lyn's heart with bubbles of maternal love. She unwrapped every baby's blanket and wiggled their toes. When she was alone, she often rocked and sang lullabies as babies drifted off to sleep. Joy Lyn looked deep into the babies' eyes and whispered how much they were loved by God and their new families.

"When are you and your husband going to start a family, Joy Lyn?" a sister asked.

"Hopefully soon. He's gone a lot and I hope I can get pregnant. So far we haven't had any luck."

"I'll pray for your miracle to arrive soon."

"Thank you, Sister."

Joy Lyn's favorite baby to rock also had the funnest name in the nursery, Mini Mink. A couple from the Air Force base had visited several times that week and inquired about adopting her. She had Caucasian features mixed with island texture and her demeanor was sweet and calm.

"We want a child and I haven't been able to get pregnant for a very long time," the wife confided to Joy Lyn. "We hope the Sisters will approve us to adopt MM. We've already fallen in love with her."

"I know what you mean. She's such a good baby. I hope to have one of my own soon." Joy Lyn couldn't hold back the longing to have a child of her own.

"You're so young, you've got plenty of time."

"I work for a family on base. If you get to adopt MM, I would love to help you out as a nanny."

"There's nothing I would love more!"

It was a moment of weakness. Logan pulled the curtains closed in a motel room across the road from a bar. He started the evening with his fishing buddies – just grabbing a beer after work. Alcohol removed his inhibitions and he found himself in the same positions he'd been in with several other girls over the past few weeks. Committed married life wasn't for him after all – although Joy Lyn had boosted his confidence more than any woman he'd known, including his mom back home in Ohio.

Dark thoughts intruded rational thinking and he was afraid. He knew there would be consequences, and actual ramifications of his infidelity had yet to be exacted.

Pepe's brother had heard rumblings of his niece's husband hanging out with prostitutes. He shook his head and looked at the bar manager.

"Has this guy been in here buying women bar passes?" Uncle asked a bartender and showed a picture of Logan around the bar.

"I see him a couple times a week here throwing around bills to take our girls out for a good time."

"You're sure you've seen him in the last five months?"

"I saw him here a couple of days ago. He buys juice for our girls pretty often."

"Hey, has this guy bought you a bar pass?" Uncle approached a scantily dressed girl seated at the bar.

No, no. But I know who he is. I heard a rumor."

"What kind of rumor?"

"My girl, June Mink, was out of work for a while because she was pregnant. She thought it was his baby."

Uncle rubbed his knotted-up knuckles into an open palm. Jail would be too good for a guy like Logan. His niece wouldn't have her name or reputation sullied by this foreign dirtbag. Not as long as she had an uncle and father to protect her. Beer from the bottom of his drink made a swooshing sound as he gulped the last of it and slammed the glass on the bar top.

⬥

When Uncle returned to his motel, he called his brother. Pepe answered on the fourth ring.

"Please don't tell me you need money," Pepe said immediately.

"Good evening to you too, brother."

"It's bedtime here. Where are you?"

"I'm still in Manila."

"Right, where in Manila? On the strip?"

"What are you doing there? Up to no good I suppose."

"How else would I find out information on Logan?"

"You're lying. Why are you there? Logan is a good man. A good husband."

"I just spoke to the bar manager at the Eager Beaver, and a young lady who worked there. Showed his picture around."

"Why would you do that?"

"I wanted to get answers for some rumors I've heard."

"What kind of rumors?"

"He's got a kid. By a prostitute from here. And he's still cheating on Joy Lyn."

"I don't believe it. I want evidence."

"The evidence is a resident of the Catholic orphanage near your house."

"The one Joy Lyn volunteers for?"

"That very one, and apparently there's a birth certificate with his name listed as the father."

"What's the baby's name?"

"Something silly. I think I heard Mini Mink."

"Come back. We need a plan. I'm going to get that son of a bitch."

⸺◈⸺

Logan knew he was dead if Joy Lyn found out he had been spending most of his hard-earned money on escorts and hotel rooms. She couldn't find out or he could be put in jail for adultery, and he had no one on his side to defend him, nor any defense.

He skipped work all together that week to hang out in bars, drink beer and work out his sexual fantasies. He felt much more comfortable in bed with girls from the Eager Beaver. They made him feel big and strong – and desirable. They let him do things to them that he would never dream of asking Joy Lyn. And he was detached from any expectations. Joy Lyn never stopped talking about having children. The only reason she wanted to have sex was to get pregnant. He had trouble performing because of the pressure.

—•—

The front door quietly clicked shut and Joy Lyn looked into the main room from her bed. Sleep was difficult when Logan was away at work. A dark figure tiptoed across the tile floor, barely making a sound. Joy Lyn reached for a big stick she had hidden under her bed, just in case, and lay quiet with her eyes barely open.

The intruder grabbed the top of a chair as he stumbled in the dark and made a squeaking noise. He stopped abruptly and froze like a statue. Joy Lynn watched the shadow in the moonlight through squinted eyes and gripped the stick under her sheets. He moaned and leaned over Joy Lyn in bed.

Her grip on the stick was solid as she cracked it over the back of the prowler's head. He cried out and fell forward as a splatter of blood hit the blanket. Joy Lyn jumped out of bed and screamed. She hit the light switch and there was her drunk and now wounded husband writhing on the bed.

"Oh my God. I thought you were a robber or rapist! she said.

"Dammit! Why did you attack me?"

"Why didn't you call out when you got home?"

Logan's head spun even more with a crack in it. Joy Lyn picked up the phone to call her mother, even though she knew she was fast asleep at home. She'd know what to do.

"Lay there. Stay down. Here, take this towel and put it on your head. You're bleeding," Joy Lyn told Logan as she dialed the phone.

"Should I take him to the hospital? I think I heard his skull crack."

"Stay calm honey, I'll send your father over to help. He'll take care of it."

⬥

Pepe and his brother responded to Joy Lyn's distress call in the wee hours of the morning and loaded Logan into the backseat of a light blue Honda Civic.

"How are you feeling back there?"

"My head is pounding, but the bleeding has stopped. Where are you taking me?"

"Joy Lyn wanted us to take you to get checked out at the hospital. You may have a concussion or something."

"Thank you. Family is everything," Logan said.

"It really is, isn't it," Uncle said.

Pepe stopped the car in a remote part of the jungle, not far from the hospital. The sky was a light pink and blue when Uncle dragged Logan into the thick brush. A rusty machete attached to his leg made Logan wince and his eyes got wide.

"You disrespected my family," Uncle said while Pepe took a walk to turn a blind eye.

"What are you talking about? I just came home drunk and Joy Lyn thought I was a bad guy!"

"You are a bad guy. The worst kind of guy. You cheat on your wife and make her and her whole family look like fools for taking you in."

"But I love Joy Lyn!"

"Not anymore, you don't. We know everything. We know about the baby in the orphanage. We know you're hanging out with hookers instead of working. You are done here."

"Please, please, don't kill me. I promise I'll leave and never come back."

"You got that right. But I need a souvenir and you need a reminder to never return."

Uncle grabbed Logan's head and wrenched it between his large bicep, holding onto his hair. He unsheathed his tarnished machete and pulled Logan's right ear out and chopped most of it off. Logan screamed bloody murder and ran into the jungle when Pepe pushed him away. Blood gushed and a trail followed Logan's tracks.

Uncle wiped the blood off of his weapon and stuck Logan's ear in the back pocket of his pants.

"Come on, Pepe! Our work is done here."

The brothers drove off into the sunrise. "Margarita is going to be upset if we miss early Mass."

Chapter 23

Moorea Please

Neve and Jenae

M oorea, Tahiti.

If Jenae and Neve couldn't resolve their disagreements in paradise, then life together would be hell anywhere else on earth. She assumed he was having tons of fun while he was away working in Tahiti for two week stretches. She hadn't seen his tiny, two-room apartment that six guys shared with bunk beds, no TV, and a barely functioning kitchen. Only four guys slept there at any one time, but rules required quiet time to accommodate everyone's schedules. They were all new pilots at the airline – getting their hours in, so they could move to a larger carrier. Two were from New Zealand and the rest were Aussies. All were counting on getting an offer to fly with an Australian airline, except for Neve. He wanted to go back to America.

News that Logan had expatriated himself from the U.S., making him a fugitive of the FBI, was sweet justice for Neve. Jenae informed him that Logan had cleared up all of his misdeeds in keeping Neve out of the country before he left, and wished them the best. Logan claimed to be a reformed man and planned to live a long, complete life with his new wife in the Philippines. Jenae had bought it, but Neve wasn't born yesterday, and he'd dealt with his share of psychopaths in the police force.

⸻◦⸻

Bank holidays weren't a thing in the U.S., but Jenae was willing to take the day off if it meant one more day with Neve in tropical Tahiti. Neve changed clothes after his last flight of the day and picked Jenae up from her gate with a flower for her hair.

"Are you ready for some lovin'?" Neve asked.

"I'm ready for you to come back and live with me full time again. But yeah, I could use some sexy-time too."

Neve looked back at his co-pilot, who had taken a long step forward toward him and Jenae.

"You really want to do this? Don't you have somewhere to go?" Neve said hoping he didn't hear the word "sexy-time" in his conversation with Jenae.

"Yeah, no problem, mate. I've got a car booked. I'm happy to take you to the ferry terminal on my way into town."

Jenae gave the co-pilot a big hug when Neve introduced her to the only other Kiwi pilot working remotely.

A baggage collector tossed their bags on a big cart that read, "Mo'orea." Neve and Jenae rode an escalator up to the loading area for their ferry ride to the island closest to Pape'ete.

"There's a snack stand over there. I'm going to grab some pineapple," Neve said.

Jenae leaned against the rail and watched their boat get bigger as it chugged closer to the dock. She breathed in fresh ocean air and wondered how she'd gotten so lucky.

"What's that red stuff?" Jenae asked.

"Paprika, or some kind of spicy mix they put on the pineapple. It's good. Try it."

Jenae licked her pink fingers, "That was good! Now I'm really hungry."

"We can get some food on the boat."

Neve sat at a large sea-sprayed window in a long booth big enough to seat eight people. Jenae carried a tray with a large fried chicken leg, a sausage roll and a small lettuce salad. She rocked back and forth with the boat, careful not to lose her grip on the bounty.

"Yum, that looks terrible. You must really be hungry." Neve side-eyed her.

"A girl's gotta eat."

"Look out there – I saw a couple of whales. It looks like a mama and a baby," Neve said.

"So cute. The water is a bit choppy out here, but look at the shore – it's clear and blue." Jenae tugged the last bit of chicken meat off of the bone with her front teeth.

High school boys seated nearby finished their mounded plates of chicken, while they laughed and cajoled. A petite girl sat by herself, with a stingray bike leaned next to her as she read a school book.

"Yeah, the kids from Moorea commute to school by ferry every day. We don't have public schools for the older kids on the island," a woman sitting across the table explained. "You'll see. It's very remote and rustic, except for the hotels for tourists."

⸺◆⸺

A cabbie loaded their luggage into the trunk and smiled and drove. She didn't speak much English and limited French. Neve had booked a room at an exclusive hotel, or so he thought.

"I swear, I have a reservation here. I have the paperwork." Neve dug into his bag and pulled out a printout of pictures of bungalows over clear turquoise waters.

"See?"

The bellman shook his head and said, "no this isn't the place. You are up the road a ways."

"Thank goodness our cab waited for us!" Jenae said.

"Can you take us here instead?" Neve pointed to the paper for the cabbie and was afraid the hotel he booked wouldn't be good enough.

She nodded kindly. "I take you. No problem."

"I can't believe you didn't know where we were staying?" Jenae snickered.

"Talking to the travel agent was so confusing. I swear I was looking at that resort. He must have redirected me to a different property at the last second," Neve said defensively.

<hr />

They didn't get an overwater bungalow, but they were right on the beach with clear blue water steps from their sun deck. A coral reef surrounded the island and created a swimming pool effect that prevented big waves from reaching shore.

"We'd like a kayak for two please." Neve pumped sunscreen out of the communal vat and rubbed it on Jenae's back. He sized-up the situation and handed Jenae a paddle while he turned the boat in the direction of the bungalows.

"This is so relaxing! I love being able to do activities with you on your days off," Jenae said as they navigated over a coral bay, and weaved between bungalow foundation poles.

"I wish you could come more often, but I get home for good stretches of time and it won't last forever."

"I get so lonely without you though," Jenae said.

Neve looked around and grinned. "I got some good news."

"What. You won the lottery?" Jenae said sarcastically.

"Close. I got interviews with two major U.S. airlines. My instructor helped me out."

"Are you joking? You better not be kidding me!"

"Yep, after I leave here, I'll fly to Australia for an in-person interview with one of them."

Jenae looked back at Neve and rocked the boat as she kneeled in the middle of the kayak.

"Are you kidding me? I'm so happy!"

She hugged Neve around the neck and pulled him off the small boat, kissing him as they plunged into calm blue bliss. They rolled around in the cool waters. Neve slowly pulled himself back onto the kayak. Schools of fish nibbled at coral, green slimy seaweed hung from ropes, Jimmy Buffet blared from the deck above her head, and bluish exhaust from a speed boat zipped by, overwhelming her senses.

"Hey, help me back up." Jenae tried to drag herself up by a paddle Neve had extended. She felt the strength of his hand wrapped around her wrist, slid on her belly and flopped into her seat.

⚬

Neve inched closer to Jenae's nose and gently kissed her lips. Jenae processed the moment, her eyes fluttered and she melted into his arms on their king-sized bed. She'd already showered and was halfway wrapped in the resort's white waffle-fabric robe with its insignia embroidered on the right chest. They spooned and napped in advance of the van pick up for their planned night out.

A big, black air-conditioned passenger van pulled into the roundabout entry at the resort. The concierge in a tropical tan and brown short sleeved shirt ushered eight guests to the opened sliding door. The first couple in line scooted to the very back row. Jenae sat directly behind the driver.

"How long is the drive to the luau?" Neve asked.

"We have one more stop to pick up two more guests. Thirty minutes at the most," the driver turned his head to project his voice to the back of the van.

"Where are you from?" Jenae asked a woman with big blonde hair and large gems on her fingers.

"We're from Canada. I've been planning this trip for a year. It's a big birthday!" her doting husband answered.

"I had to convince my brother to take over the business while we're gone for three weeks," the birthday girl said.

"Oh, what do you do?" Jenae asked.

"I'm a house husband. My whole existence is taking care of my beautiful wife."

Neve started to twirl a tuft of hair on the front of his head and smirked. Jenae nudged him with her elbow but he kept his head down.

A bend in the road around a large bay slowed the van down to twenty miles per hour. The sun set behind low clouds above the blue ocean, and back-glowed palm leaves along the road.

"This is one of the larger towns on the island. I grew up here," the driver said.

"Look out there! That's our cruise ship. We'll spend a week on it touring islands starting next week," Canadian house husband declared.

Unloaded guests were served orange beverages, which was placed on a pink and white hibiscus print fabric. A vivacious older couple serenaded from a log bench alongside a wooden plank walkway. He wore a green woven hat and vigorously played the ukulele and sang. She wore a flowered headpiece, and kept beat with her right hand on a tall, wooden drum that she held upright with her bare feet. Neither of their legs were long enough to touch the ground. Guests sipped and wandered around dirt pathways of a Polynesian wonderland. Historical buildings housed very old wooden boats and outriggers. But Jenae was most intrigued by the beautiful flowers and plants along the way. Most guests had taken their seats in an outdoor arena by the time Neve and Jenae found their way to the gathering place – barely in time for the show.

"Excusez moi. Excusez moi," Jenae said, stumbling over bare toes in flip flops as they made their way to seats stuck at the end of the row next to a wood and straw wall.

"Pardon, merci. Pardon, merci," Neve parroted behind her.

Heritage of Tahiti was on display as a large, round Tahitian man narrated the ceremony. He was dressed in a black wrap skirt, tropical shirt, and a woven hat that resembled the statue of liberty crown. He guided two other muscular men to uncover an earth oven that he called ahima'a. Those men wore the same garb except with a more modest head wrap. The festive meal for the evening (or tama'ara'a) had been smoked in that oven where the pig had roasted for many hours. A mainly French audience squealed in amazement as the dinner was revealed.

"Seems a lot like a Hawaiian luau," Jenae said.

"Only they speak French and Tahitian," Neve said.

A teaser dance and enactment by the same men entertained guests in the arena as they waited for their turn to be called to go through the buffet of seafood appetizers. Tables were adorned with seashell candle holders, a woven divider, and a local potted plant in the middle. Wine glasses held folded red fabric napkins that matched a red and white tropical table runner. Palm fronds hung from the rafters of a well-built structure made to look like a big hut.

Frenchmen sat at multiple tables with other Frenchmen, Spanish speakers sat together, and a Japanese group had three full tables. Jenae and Neve sat at the only English-speaking table, and only six out of ten seats were taken. A couple from California became fast friends with them and provided the only conversation all evening. A South African couple kept to themselves and smiled and nodded at inappropriate moments.

"I can't eat this seafood. It looks raw."

It's not technically raw, it's been cooked in citrus. Acid cooked ceviche," Neve explained.

"My stomach is upset. I'll wait for the main course." Jenae excused herself to the toilet.

Roasted pork didn't appeal to Jenae's stomach either, but she managed to put down pastries topped with berries and cream. She strategically finished early and positioned herself to get first dibs on seating for the main show. Neve and Jenae sat front and center on the second bleacher.

Heat from fire torches warmed their faces. Four barely dressed native men spun double sided torches to drums playing in the background. They whistled and whooped, "Hey!" as they flexed their abs to keep the fire sticks spinning. Naked glutes and tattooed thighs danced less than ten feet from their seats. Dancers wore what looked like grass skirts on their calves, upper arms and neck. But mere G-strings held up a washcloth sized brown cloth draped over their loins.

"Did you see that? I just saw that guy's big balls." Jenae covered her mouth and turned to Neve.

"Probably did. I'm not sure there's any coverage under that dishtowel."

—◆O◆—

A big bus had been waiting outside the show. Their driver ate a plate of food at the side of the bus, while passengers loaded for the thirty-to-forty-minute ride back to their hotels.

"Hey, our driver has the Statue of Liberty straw hat on. Like the guy at the food pit," Jenae said.

"I think that is the same guy. Teamwork makes the dream work. Manpower is limited on an island like this," Neve replied.

Jenae greeted their American friends who sat behind them on the bus. She was extra attentive, as it was her last chance to socialize with an American for a while. As they drove along, she couldn't stop thinking about what it would be like living back in California, or Texas or even Kansas.

"See ya later San Fran!" Jenae shouted too loud.

The couple looked back and waved.

—◦—

Neve snuck back into the room the next morning. "I got you a baguette from the store down the road." He handed Jenae a latte in a porcelain cup from the restaurant.

"Oh good. I'm starving. I just couldn't handle what they were serving last night. Traveler's stomach or something."

"Bread is the only thing I can afford on this island, only because the French government subsidizes it."

"Oh yeah! That makes sense. Have you read Les Miserables?"

"No, but I remember you went to the musical in San Francisco with psycho Logan," Neve said.

"That was a really bad time for us. He seems to have gotten himself out of a big mess by escaping to the Philippines."

"I just hope he doesn't bother us anymore. Put your suit on, I want you to go snorkeling with me."

"So, this is how the other half lives. Or a tiny portion of the other half." They donned their masks and slipped on flippers in shallow beach water.

"Enjoy it while you can. The future holds no promises, only challenges," Neve said as he laid down gently in the water and pulled Jenae by the hand. They smiled with their eyes at each other while breathing through their snorkels. Fins moved slowly in rhythm and Jenae pointed to fish along the way. Their connection was deepening through nature, synchronicity and beauty. Floating together in a massive ocean, with joined hands and hearts, meant conquering the world wouldn't be so bad after all, as long as they had each other.

Chapter 24

Pinatubo Pressure
Logan - Neve and Jenae

I t could have been mistaken for a terrible car accident. Sirens, trucks speeding, muffled voices on a megaphone from a cop car. The only thing missing was the crash. Logan looked out a window from his hospital bed on the second floor. For a moment, he worried Pepe had sent the police to arrest him for adultery – maybe half an ear wasn't enough punishment for degrading Joy Lyn's reputation.

He needed a night in clean white sheets after the emergency room doctor sewed him up the night before. Pain from his half-gone ear made him forget about his concussion. His head throbbed and eyes burned but his stomach rumbled when he smelled a small bowl of pineapple on his breakfast tray.

"Nurse, when do I have to leave?" Logan rubbed his forehead.

"Your doctor will be making rounds this morning. I would guess you have another day of IV antibiotics before he'll let you go."

"My head is pounding. Can I get something for the pain?"

"I can get you some Tylenol, but no narcotics because you are on a concussion protocol."

"I'll take whatever I can get."

"Sure, I'll bring some in with your other meds."

More sirens passed by – heading inland. The nurse looked out the window with concern.

"I thought those were ambulances, but they aren't stopping at the hospital."

"I felt my bed shake this morning. Was there an earthquake?" The shuddering reminded him of San Francisco.

"I'll ask the administrator, she'll know. In fact, she'll be coming in to talk to you about your injuries. How did they happen?"

"I can't remember much, but I got jumped at a bar last night. One guy hit me on the head with a bat, and then I woke up bleeding from my ear."

"You're lucky you made it to the hospital."

◆○◆

Family dinner after church had an empty seat next to Joy Lyn, and an extra serving of quietness. She hid her puffy eyes behind an embroidered handkerchief held up by both hands. Joy Lyn's silent body convulsions from crying were hardly noticeable due to her tiny physique. She was embarrassed by the stories that her uncle had told her. Logan was supposed to be building a future for the two of them together. And she held his baby, Mini Mink. Her whole future was ruined in one bad night.

A voice from a slow-moving cop car said something about an earthquake and an eruption.

"Warning! Warning! You are under orders to evacuate. Mount Pinatubo is active. It could blow at any moment."

Pepe wandered out the front door to flag the officer down. He turned around and waved Margarita back inside.

"I'll find out what's going on. You stay with Joy Lyn."

"We've had a couple of big earthquakes and they're worried that it will set the volcano off. But we don't know when."

"Pepe wasn't so sure. But dogs running erratically through the neighborhood knew something was wrong. Monkeys talked in the jungle nearby.

⸺◆⸺

Logan's phone rang. He moved the tissue box aside to pick up the receiver. His boat crew buddy had heard that he was in the hospital and was more amused than concerned.

"Are you still alive?"

Logan closed his eyes and thought about the assaults – unintentional by Joy Lyn and on purpose by her uncle. He felt a pang of guilt and sadness for losing Joy Lyn.

"I'm still kicking. My doctor said I can leave tomorrow morning. Do you have room on your couch?"

"I do, if you promise to come work on my fishing boat with me when you're all healed up."

———⬥———

The couch at his buddy's place seemed less and less safe with each shake of the earth. Warnings about evacuation were coming more frequently as magma slowly rose in the volcano's underbelly.

A flier was left on the doorstep to get out. It read, *Mt. Pinatubo could do one of three things: reduce its seismic activity, remain at the same level for weeks, or quickly increase activity (indicating an imminent eruption) and pose an immediate life-threatening situation to Clark Air Base and the local community.*

"On Sunday, June 9th, seismic activity increased over the safe threshold, indicating the likelihood of a major eruption within the next 24 hours. At 2315, the decision to evacuate Clark was announced." Logan heard those warnings on a radio next to his pillow.

The 50-mile exodus from Clark on a two-lane road to Subic Bay began at 0600 on June 10th. Air Force personnel and their families made the four hour bumper-to-bumper trip through the mountains. Threats directed against Americans by the communist New People's Army complicated the evacuation and required U.S. Navy and Marine helicopters to fly overhead as a precautionary measure.

Logan was far away from Clark Air Force Base, and felt safe because the military evacuated 16,000 people to Subic Bay, which was very close to him. Officials quickly warned that it was in critical danger with a doubled population. It left very few options.

Navy and Marine Corps families shared their small base homes with two and three Air Force families. Other evacuees slept on mattresses in the two base chapels, the day care center, school classrooms, and any corner that could fit a temporary bed. Almost the entire Department of Defense population in the Philippines was out of danger . . . until the pressure released.

Overcrowding at Subic Bay severely strained water and food supply, prompting a decision to evacuate all Air Force dependent personnel to the United States. No one knew it at the time, but that quick decision was a major safety measure. It allowed the Navy to steam fleet assets to Subic Bay a full 24 hours before a catastrophic eruption.

"Are you getting out of here? Do you really think Pinatubo will blow? Logan asked a bartender as he watched a talking head on the television hanging above a wall of liquor bottles.

"Some Philippine politicians and media criticized the decision to evacuate, saying that it was politically, not safety motivated, and based on an attempt by the United States to obtain an advantage in upcoming base extension negotiations," blared from the TV.

"I stay out of politics. I got no opinion. Go if you want to go. I heard ships are being brought in to take military and ex-pats to Cebu."

"Where's that?" Logan said.

"About 350 miles south. It takes a full day on a ship to get there."

"Then what?"

"Eh, I heard there will be planes from there."

Logan stopped at the men's room to take a leak in a big metal trough. He pissed on one end and watched his bodily fluid flow down to a drain pipe that wasn't attached to outdoor pipes. It just splashed on the floor and got his feet wet.

"Seems appropriate," Logan mumbled to himself.

⸺◆⸺

On Friday, the fourteenth, the first major ash fell on Subic Bay. In the evening, rain and ash mixed together, forming a heavy, sticky substance that made roads extremely slick. By early Saturday morning, it looked as if it had a light dusting of snow.

Logan flashed back to his more pleasant childhood memories of sledding down a hill in a neighbor's yard in the real stuff. But ash is not snow. Even if the volcano didn't fully blow, the highly conductive nature of the volcanic ash was already playing havoc on power distribution and the water supply system.

"Black Saturday" began at approximately 0930. A spectacular ash plume, clearly visible from Subic Bay, rose hundreds of feet into the air. The major eruption that many volcanologists predicted had finally arrived. All had agreed that Subic Bay would receive ash, but far more fell than any volcanologists had predicted in their worst-case scenario. At the same time, Typhoon Yunya was racing across the island of Luzon near both bases. One volcanologist said it was a "ten-million-to-one shot" that a volcano would erupt, after lying dormant for more than 600 years – and coupled with a typhoon. This catastrophic combination radically shifted winds, causing destructive forces that no one could have predicted.

By noon, all base power was lost. Nature was totally in control. Falling ash blocked out all sunlight, reducing visibility to zero. Earthquakes in excess of 5.0 on the Richter scale made jelly out of the already shaking terrain.

⊰•◦✦◦•⊱

Operation Fiery Vigil saved Logan, but not his family. American ships docked and quickly loaded families and civilians who looked American.

"Sir, I'm going to need to see some ID to let you on the ship," a seaman stopped Logan.

"All of my legal papers were destroyed under the ash. Please let me pass," Logan said.

"Check with that table over there. They can check for your name on our State Department documents."

"Logan saluted the seaman and looked back at him while he skirted around the check point and swiftly found himself a seat in the corner of the ship.

Before he knew it, Logan was safely on his 350-mile voyage to the southern Philippine island of Cebu. His boat was a converted warship that had been quickly converted to a cruise ship. Sailors gave up their racks for the evacuees. Menus included hotdogs and potato chips for the children and first-class lounges became playrooms.

Logan thought about what Mini Mink would look like when she grew up old enough to play games of jump rope like children on this ship. *Could she possibly be here with her new parents? I hope she finds someone better than me to raise her. God knows she had no future with June Mink.* He thought.

Pet motels were created out of boxes, not only for dogs and cats but a pet wolf too; and rubber gloves were used as baby bottles. A baby was born on the ship and was named Abraham in honor of Abraham Lincoln. An elderly-man almost converted Logan when he described this experience as living the end of the world, as described in the Book of Revelations.

After evacuees completed their 19-hour trip to Cebu, helicopters moved them from ships to Mactan International Airport. Most met Air Force transports that took them to their first stop in Guam, and eventual transport to the United States.

"Are there any flights to Australia?" Logan asked a relief worker in the terminal."

"We're waiting for the RAAF to come, but the New Zealand government has sent a plane to take citizens back home."

"Yeah, even better mate."

⸰⸰⸰

For six hours Neve laid by the phone in anticipation. He couldn't sleep, but didn't want to wake her in the middle of the night. The excitement to tell Jenae about interviews he'd set up at two major airlines in America kept his head spinning. A water kettle boiled next to a partially chipped tea cup with a bag of Earl Grey set in its base.

"Burrt, burrt. Burrt, burrt."

"Hello?"

"Good morning, sweetheart. Did I wake you?"

"Maybe a little bit, but I'm up now. When are you coming home?"

"I hope your visit here was fun enough to sustain you, it may have been your last one for a while. I'm going to interview with two U.S. airlines next week."

Jenae sat up on the side of the bed and leaned forward.

"When did this happen?"

"There was a change of plans because of the volcano erupting in the Philippines."

"Wait, what volcano.?"

"You haven't been watching the news?"

"The news is different here, and hit or miss. I only watch at dinnertime."

"So, Mount Pinatubo in the Philippines erupted a few days ago, and the ash is causing flight issues in the area. They evacuated a bunch of people on ships, and the military is moving an entire base back to the States."

"I wondered why we had such good sunsets here lately. The sky is deep orange at dusk."

Jenae laid back down and looked out her window on the winter hues of Hagley Park.

"I don't want to spend too much money on this phone call, so I'll get to the point. I'm flying out to California today."

"For how long?"

"A week or maybe ten days. It depends."

"I could meet you there! It's been so cold and rainy here since I left Tahiti."

"I wish you could, but I don't think we can afford it. And I'll be stressed out interviewing. I don't want to screw this up. It's my only chance."

"You think I'd screw it up?"

"No, no, no. I would be distracted because I love you so much. And besides, you've been looking forward to your work retreat in the mountains. Aren't you going skiing?"

"Yeah, I guess I can't skip out on that. But I'm really homesick. And I'm really Neve sick."

"Me too honey."

"You better get this job! I hate living apart."

"I'll do my best. Go back to bed. I'll let you know when I land in San Francisco."

"Good luck honey and safe travels."

She was excited for Neve, but sad for herself. Her big life in New Zealand had turned back into a small life. She loved the country and the people, but missed her country and her people.

Chapter 25

Slippery Slopes

Jenae - Neve

Jenae and Fiona were the car service for work's winter retreat on the South Island. Most of their workmates had never been skiing at Mt. Hutt before because it was more of a local's ski hill. Flynn avoided booking in the mountains near pricey Queenstown. It was more affordable and transportation was free. Airport pick up was easy since most were on the same flight from the North Island. Jenae had already stopped at her favorite deli for a tray of snacks and had drinks in a cooler in the back of her car. She played her favorite cassette tape, Garth Brooks, and sang along out loud for an unappreciative captive audience.

Gerry navigated Fiona's car as if he'd been there before. Which he had, just two weeks before.

"You two see each other more than I see my husband," Jenae said."

"Ah, you'll be alright Jenae. We'll distract you with a fun ski weekend."

The caravan of cars made their way into the Southern Alps to a town called Methven. A lodge accommodated the entire group with room to spare. Although the pool and golf course were closed for winter, Jenae and Fiona shared a room with a magnificent view of snow-covered Mt. Hutt just outside their picture window. Fiona had called ahead to finagle the best room.

Flynn had some leeway on his budget for dinner and activities because of his frugal choices for location and accommodation. The team met at the hotel bar and had two large tables set up for them in the dining room. Appetizers were ordered for the table while they looked at the menu and ordered beer and wine for dinner.

"I guess I'll try the lamb," Jenae ordered.

"Ugh, I hate lamb. I'll have the local fish, please," Fiona said.

"How can you hate your country's biggest export?"

"I don't hate it. I've just eaten so much that I'm tired of it right now."

"I get that." Jenae passed her menu down the line where their waitress collected them in a pile.

"Be right back with your drinks," the server said.

"So tell me, how are you and Gerry getting on?" Jenae asked.

"What, with our sex life?" Fiona asked.

"No. Of course not. Are the two of you serious?"

"We like each other very much, but we haven't said the love word to each other yet."

Jenae pushed her bottom lip out in disappointment and made a sad hum.

"I mean, we're kind of on a plateau. Traveling on an airplane to see each other is a big barrier. And I don't know if I want to move to the North Island to be with him."

Gerry walked up behind the gossiping girls and took his seat next to Fiona.

"I've never skied before. I was just asking Flynn if we could take lessons. He said our marketing manager was going to teach us beginners," Gerry said.

"When did he get so cheap with the company's money?" Jenae asked.

"I think he's trying to meet a budget target. He must be up for a promotion," Fiona said.

White exhaust puffed out of a coach bus while the driver placed bags of supplies underneath. Flynn's team peered out the front windows of the lodge as they gathered coats, gloves and hats for the ride up the mountain.

"Spread out on both sides of the bus. You'll understand why when we get to the curvy steep bits of the mountain," Flynn joked. Except he wasn't joking about the harrowing drive up an icy one and a half lane road with a sheer cliff and no guard rails. Jenae sat on the outside edge and tried not to look down and imagine their bus in a ball of fire at the bottom of the mountain. Fear of heights sent her into immediate prayer for safe delivery to the top. Her prayers were answered.

Jenae never liked the cold, but she had to act excited for the company. She and Fiona were diplomats for the South Island and Jenae pretended skiing was her favorite winter pass time. Colorado excursions to the Rocky Mountains in her high school years with her church group were more of a social retreat than an outdoor passion. "Tree bashing" in fresh powder was her favorite because although it looked dangerous it really wasn't. Six inches of fluffy snow kept their speed down and gave cover for the occasional bared-ass bathroom break.

"The boots hurt," Jenae looked up as she closed the second bracket on her left foot.

"They need to be extra tight so your ankles don't move, or you could break a bone," the equipment helper explained.

Novice skiers headed to the bunny hill for a speedy, ski lesson. A four-person chair lift just beyond the magic carpet moved swiftly to the top of the mountain. Scotty lined up next to Jenae to ride up together with Flynn and Fiona.

"Here Scotty, you take the outside seat. You can push off on the arm rest at the top." Jenae scooted around Scotty's skis and tried not to sit next to her, but the next chair was coming fast.

"Thanks, Jenae. I'll try not to drag you down at the top," Scotty said with a chuckle.

"Look outside and grab the bar to steady the seat before you sit." Jenae rolled her eyes. The chair swung back and forth as their skis lifted off the ground and they adjusted their weight on the hanging couch.

A group behind them started an echo chant. "Aaay - yo – ay, ay, ay – yo." Flynn looked down to the slope below, past dangling skis attached to agonizing boots. Fiona turned backward when they hollered again into the mountain, "Aaay - yo – ay, ay, ay – yo." She responded with Jenae, "Aaay - yo – ay, ay, ay – yo." and rocked the chair with a Jamaican rhythm and giggled.

As the slick ramp at the top of the mountain came into view, Flynn spoke up.

"OK, Scotty and Fiona, you two veer off to your sides. Jenae and I will take the middle lanes."

Scotty's trouble standing up predictably became the group's problem. The extra time it took for Scotty to stand up made her turn with the chair and run over the back of Jenae's skis as she escaped down the mountain. Scotty fell in the middle of the exit ramp, and tried to scramble away in an army crawl on her hands and knees with her legs splayed. The next chair whipped around before the lift operator could slow it down, and the skiers dismounted into a heap of coats and hats on top of Scotty.

Flynn and Fiona watched from below and laughed and yelled, "Aaay - yo – ay, ay, ay – yo!"

Morning ski session was short and sweet, and Jenae was happy to release the pressure of the top strap off of her ankle. The team met for an overpriced lunch and tall tales on an outdoor sunny deck at the ski lodge. Steam from Fiona's paper cup of hot tea warmed her lips and her red cheeks glowed.

"How did your ski lessons go?" She asked Gerry.

"Good, but I missed being with you."

"You're sweet." Fiona leaned in and gave him a side hug. She'd never been in love before and wasn't sure this was it. How would she know?

"Can I get your attention please?" Flynn shouted above simmering conversations.

"I got a really good report from corporate. Our marketing manager just informed me that our novice skiers are ready to take the big boy lifts to the top of the mountain!"

"Yay! But boo! When are we going to hear about our bonuses? Did we win the competition for the most sales?" "I'll address that tonight after dinner. But after you finish lunch, we're all going to the top of the mountain together for a group bonding activity."

Talk in the ladies' bathroom after lunch buzzed about bonuses. Jenae felt nauseated after her chicken and bean soup.

"Excuse me, does anyone have a Pepto? I feel like I'm going to blow chow." A stranger reached in her bag and offered her a couple of Tums.

"Thanks, cheers."

"Is everyone here? We are going to ski down this mountain together. I'm the leader and I want all of my new skiers behind me. The rest of you fall into place. The key is to get into snow plow position and interlock with the person in front of you. We're going to look like a giant caterpillar as we glide side to side down the mountain," the marketing manager with strong thigh muscles announced.

Whoops and hollers filled the mountainside as the group leaned on each other, guided, and gave way to get down together. Fiona locked in behind Scotty. Her bountiful bottom kept the rest of the line of skiers steady.

"That was so much fun!" Jenae fist bumped Scotty at the bottom of the hill.

<hr>

Clink, clink, clink. Flynn stood at the head of the long wooden table after dessert was served.

"Can I have your attention, please? I have announcements to make."

The volume of conversation around the table lowered a tiny decibel.

Clink, clink, clink, clink. Clink.

"I've got good news!"

The room went silent as he walked over to a brown cardboard box and set it on his chair. The marketing manager pulled bottles of brut champagne from a kettle filled with ice.

And waitresses carried trays with empty champagne flutes that had frosted lettering on the side.

"I'm here to announce that our team not only reached our goal but we outperformed every other team along the way! Once everyone has a full glass of champagne in their hand, we'll toast."

The room cheered with the news as champagne corks flew over the tables.

"Cheers to the best team I've ever led!" Flynn shouted.

"Cheers!" The team returned in unison as they clinked glasses.

A basket of gift-wrapped items and envelopes were placed on the dining table. One for each employee. Flynn called each team member to the front of the room to receive their reward and a few kind words. A photographer took pictures of big smiles and the obligatory handshake.

"Jenae gets the reward for canvassing every single doctor for two quarters straight. She even found one in prison . . . just kidding. He was out by then. To your American-made tenacity. Cheers!"

"And to your enthusiastic leadership, Flynn. You are a delight to work with. Congratulations!" Jenae said in return.

Jenae had packed up her car with suitcases and leftover snacks after the team's final hike the next morning. The mountain side was muddy and too sloppy for a half day adventure as planned. She looked forward to lying on her couch in front of the TV after she dropped off her co-workers at the airport. It didn't matter what boring sport was playing in the warmth from the winter sun, as long as it put her to sleep.

<hr>

"I finally reached you," Neve sounded excited and irritated on an expensive call from California."

"Hi! I miss you. How'd your interviews go?" Jenae rubbed her eyes open as she gained full consciousness.

"I think the first one went really well. They said I would hear about an offer in a couple of weeks," Neve said.

"Congratulations! I know you got it. I mean you are the cream of the crop. They'd be so lucky to have you," Jenae gushed.

"Thanks sweetheart. I know you aren't biased at all. I appreciate your support."

"When are you coming back?"

"The other airline can't interview me until next week. I'll probably be gone for another eight days." Neve braced himself for her response.

"You'll be in California for two weeks? Why didn't you take me with you! I'm so homesick," Jenae's eyes filled with tears and she rested her head on her arm lain on the kitchen table. "I've been here a year, and you've been away more than home for the past six months."

"I know, I'm sorry, but you're busy with your work too."

"When are you coming home?" she said.

"I would come home tomorrow and skip the second interview, but I don't want to shoot myself in the foot by counting on just one airline."

"Alright, I guess I can wait another week. I'm going shopping though. The longer you're away, the more I'm going to purchase."

"You might be spending a lot of time at the mall then. Here's the other thing. I'm going to have to go directly back to Tahiti for my two weeks of work this month."

"Are you kidding me? That means we will be apart for six weeks?"

"We're almost halfway through it. Hang in there. I'll be checking on you. Maybe you can go to a movie with my mom or my sisters to fill the time."

"Yeah, whatever." She sniffed and wiped her nose. "I gotta go."

"I'll be back before you know it. Don't be too sad, Jenae."

"Bye." She could only get one word out and set the receiver down before she burst into a full guttural cry. She had a good cry in the fetal position on their bed until she fell back asleep at early nightfall.

Chapter 26

Escape Artist

Logan

Serendipitous opportunities are rare. And Logan wasn't afraid to follow the lot of luck that he'd been given. The only flight to New Zealand was chartered to Christchurch on the South Island, because they needed to return service members to an army base there. Logan's accent was good enough to fool the station manager once he explained that he'd picked up a different accent in the Philippines and lost his paperwork in the eruption. He got a seat courtesy of the New Zealand government relief operation.

The pilot announced that flight time would be ten hours and seven minutes until touchdown in Christchurch.

"This is not our usual route, but we are happy to be helping our government and fellow citizens out by bringing them to safety," the captain said over the speaker.

Logan's bag of money that he smuggled into the country a year ago was largely intact. He'd only spent half of it and had ten grand left in U.S currency. Most of it had been spent on

Joy Lyn and her family. He'd helped with some renovations on the family home, and bought them a new refrigerator. Pangs of regret filled his gut for leaving. But that was overridden by a wave of relief knowing that he'd escaped the responsibility of a child, hadn't been killed by his in-laws, and wouldn't be jailed for adultery.

A final destination address was required to secure the flight over and so he wrote down the one he had etched in his mind. It was Neve's residence from his visa application packet that Logan had mulled over in his mind day after day for a full year – 05 St. Albans Street. *I doubt that SOB, Neve, lives there anymore, but I'm going to check it out anyway. I hope he and Jenae broke it off.*

Two meals and a long nap was all the time it took to be transported into a more forgiving world. He ate and slept as much as he could on the plane and formulated a plan for his future in New Zealand. After touchdown, chimes from above sounded when the seatbelt sign was turned off. His fellow passengers stood up and stretched. The guy in front of him twisted at the waist left and right and looked Logan up and down before an eye-to-eye exchange was made. Logan looked away.

Logan stepped out into the aisle and opened the overhead compartment to retrieve his bag. He looked down at his shoes as he waited in the long line ahead of him to depart the plane. The young man looked his way again. Logan smiled.

"Hey man, is there a bar nearby the airport?" Logan asked.

"There are a couple of hotels close by. Pretty sure they have bars and restaurants."

"Right on. Thanks man."

"So were you in the Philippines long? I just went over to help with the rescue mission. I didn't get to see much."

"Yeah, yeah, yeah. I was there long enough to get married, and divorced. Didn't see any reason to stay after my place was crushed under all of that ash and rain, that turned it to concrete." Logan chuckled and nodded for approval.

"You married a Filipino girl?"

"Yeah, unfortunately I didn't get along too well with her uncle." He pulled on his hair to hide a large band aid covering his severed ear. "It's been a while since I've been back to the South Island. I'll need to figure things out," Logan said.

"If you want, I can leave you my work number. Just in case of an emergency."

"Thanks man. Bungee Adventures, huh. Sounds like a lot of fun." Logan took the business card from him and looked at it before shoving it into his wallet.

"It is. Come by if you are in the area, it's not too far from here. It's where commercial bungee jumping started."

"Hey man, would you mind coming with me to the currency exchange? I don't have any ID on me from the volcano and I need to get some New Zealand dollars," Logan asked the stranger.

"I guess I can show you where it is."

"Thanks man, I owe ya."

Logan used his new friend as the front man to exchange his money at the window at the airport. A solid hundred bucks for the favor was worth it for both of them.

The duffle bag on his back was lighter than usual with just money inside. Logan had dumped his gun in the ocean on his way to the boat and he was wearing most of his clothes. He picked up a map of the city and made a plan. Marivale Mall was just down the street from Neve's address, and Logan needed to buy clothes to fit in with the locals. Flip flops and tropical shirts weren't going to suffice in wintry Christchurch, New Zealand.

Skies were dim and gray, and he pushed the fog out of the way as he walked to a taxi station on the curb at the airport.

"Where to, mate?" the cabbie asked.

"I need to go shopping. I see Marivale Mall has quite a few shops from this brochure I picked up."

"It's good as gold. How was your flight? Did you come in on that rescue flight?"

"From the Philippines, yeah. I'm grateful that the government was there for us. I lost everything." Logan put on a pathetic sad face that he had practiced many times in the mirror.

"Aw, sorry about that. It must have been a big eruption –
our skies are darker at sunset. They say it's from Mt. Pinatubo.
Do you have a place to go after shopping?"

"Oh yeah, I have friends that are willing to put me up until
I get my feet on the ground again."

"Good on ya. I'll let you off just here at the front. Here's my
card. Call me if you need a ride somewhere. There is a hostel
downtown just in case."

"Ta!" Logan paid the amount on the meter and looked at the
card with a picture of a yellow taxi on the front. He waved as
the cabbie drove off in the mist and ducked into the mall.

Logan sang quietly to himself to music that softly wafted
from overhead speakers. Sure the songs were a version
of elevator music, but the jams from the seventies made
him happy and reminded him of America. A decent sized
department store sold jeans and sweatshirts. Based on what he
saw other men wearing in the store, he picked dark colored
T-shirts, one striped polo shirt and a black knit hat that covered
his injured ear.

"Do you sell shoes and belts?" he asked a girl folding shirts
on a table. She pointed to the far corner of the store.

"Yep, men's shoes are in that direction. The clearance rack is
on the back wall."

"Ta." Logan smelled his armpits and combed his hair with
his fingers at a full-length mirror hanging on the wall.

He stood in line with a cart full of items for his new
wardrobe and found deodorant and 2 in 1 shampoo and

conditioner in baskets at the front. First stop was the public toilet where he washed his face and pits and talked to himself in the mirror to hype up his confidence.

"You can do this. You can convince anyone of anything. You look good! You look hot with that tanned, fit body."

He kissed his right bicep then his left and clicked his tongue with a smile as he stood in front of the mirror.

His duffle bag was packed to the gills, so he threw his airplane outfit from the Philippines into the trash. He licked his fingers and stroked his eyebrows from the inside out and bent his neck left and then right. Pop, pop.

• ◦ •

St. Albans street was in the next neighborhood over and number 05 was really close to the main road. He was stunned that he was looking at Neve's home. His fantasy was coming true and his heart raced in his chest. He casually strolled on a cement path past the two-story house and saw a shadow in an upstairs room. It was a woman with grey hair closing the curtains. She walked away and so did Logan.

"Hello, yes. I was wondering if you could pick me up and take me to the hostel you were telling me about. I'll be at the mall where you dropped me off. Thanks. See you soon." Logan had chickened out from knocking on the front door and asking about Neve. His rumbling stomach took control over all of his other needs, and he opted for a take-out order of fish and chips with extra vinegar, and tomato sauce for the chips.

Hostel check in had begun and indeed they had an available bed. The cab driver told him that it was the best accommodations for the price and was close to everything he'd need downtown. Logan felt at home and used the microwave in the kitchen to heat up his dinner. A cold IPA from the liquor store paired nicely with fish and fries. Two blokes from the North Island played pool with him in the main room until he excused himself for an early turn down.

The bed was lumpy and a heavy wool blanket left him with hives on the soft underside of his arms, but Logan had no trouble sleeping for fourteen hours straight. Beep, beep, beep. Trash trucks rumbled through the alley below the opened sleeping room window.

"Damn, it's cold in here," another traveler said as he crawled out from the warm cocoon of his bunkbed in whitey-tighties. He hopped to the bathroom down the hallway for a piss.

Logan shut out the cold and noise with a slam of the old wooden window, which didn't stir the other two men sleeping on the other side of the room. He climbed back under his covers after his own trip to the toilet, and thought about his next moves, and Jenae.

Purple walls painted with impressionist yellow and orange flowers adorned a classic hippie-vibe coffee shop that he recognized all too well from San Francisco.

"I'll have a coffee, black, please." Logan looked over the glass case of food offerings and pointed to the scones. "I'll have a blueberry scone, too."

"Cool. Do you want it warmed up?" the cashier asked.

"You know, if you can warm it up, I'll take a chocolate chip muffin instead. Thanks." Logan found a table next to the front window with cold iron framed chairs with wooden seats. He pulled out a business card, Bungee Adventures. Louis Monro. *Huh, that sounds like a white guy name for a native islander. He looked Maori to me. I should go out and visit the outfit.*

"Hey man, do you know how far the bungee bridge is from here?" Logan asked.

"Most of them are down by Queenstown. Looks like this is on the Kawarau Bridge down there. I think it's the original bungee jumping bridge."

"Have you ever jumped?"

"Not yet. It's too expensive and scary for me. Maybe one day I'll work up the courage."

"I think I'm going to try it," Logan said.

"You'll need a car to get down there."

"I'm going to wander over to the used car lot later today, and see if I can afford something. Guess I'll be here awhile."

"Good on ya. They have some good deals around the corner. They import used cars from Japan because the steering wheel is on the left side too."

Logan opened the local newspaper to the back pages where used compact cars were advertised within his budget. "I'll let you know how the negotiation goes."

<hr>

"What are you looking for?" a slick and handsome car salesman asked as Logan walked slowly through the lot.

"Ah, something economical and reliable," Logan said.

"We've got a few of those on this lot. We just got a new shipment from Japan."

"Lots of Toyotas and Hondas. My father-in-law had a Civic back in the Philippines. I think I'll go with a Toyota."

"We have compacts and four-door sedans. Do you care what color?"

"You have a lot of white cars. I don't mind white."

"This two-door compact has a hatchback – it looks sporty."

"Can you knock a couple hundred off of it if I pay cash?"

"Why don't you take it for a test drive first. To see if it feels good and drives like you want."

"OK."

"I'll get the keys."

The pair took off around downtown and checked the turn radius to make sure the CV joints were good. Logan was surprised that he remembered how to drive a stick shift. He drove his mom's manual car when he was in high school but had never driven on the left side of the road. First, second, third, fourth gear felt more powerful with each shift.

"Careful! Don't forget to look right, left, right. Traffic will hit you from the right first if you pull out."

"Got it. This is a fun car!" Logan said.

"Do you want to buy this one, or look at some others? I don't want to pressure you. The only thing I care about is finding the right fit for you."

"If you can give me the right price, I think this car will do just fine."

"When we get back, I'll check with my manager to see if he'll give you a discount. You have cash, right?"

"Yep. All cash."

Logan ran his fingers on the paint around the car while the slick sales guy went inside a painted brown shed to consult with his manager. After a cup of tea and a long discussion with his manager about weekend plans, he came back out with a discount.

"Sticker price is $2,750 for this compact, which is a steal, but my manager said I could give it to you for $2,500 because you are paying cash."

"I don't have that much on me. Make it $2,200 and I'll drive it off the lot today," Logan responded.

"OK, I'll have to take the hit for that, but we have a deal."

It was refreshing for Logan to shake hands again. Ending the negotiation was also the end of a short bromance.

⬥

Since the weather was extra cold and rainy, it was best to hunker down at the hostel for a few nights before looking for work in Queenstown. Driving around town and into the countryside made Logan feel alive again. He could do what he wanted, when he wanted, to whoever he wanted. St. Albans Street was a route he used five times on the first day of sightseeing the city. He wanted to catch Neve in the driveway or yard. He hadn't seen anybody until later that evening. It was the old lady.

Knock, knock, knock.

Chapter 27

Dear Fiona

Jenae - Neve

She got a call that Flynn was in town at the last minute and he wanted to go over numbers with her. He had some marketing materials with him too, so meeting her at her condo would be easiest. He knew she didn't know yet.

"Yeah, come on up." Jenae pressed the number 9 on her phone to make the front door buzz and unlock the heavy glass door of the condo entryway for Flynn. He propped the door open with his bum and slid two cardboard boxes into the lobby. He looked at himself in the mirror and wiped his face with bare palms then pressed the up button. On the second to the top floor, he pushed the boxes out of the elevator with his feet. He'd never been to Jenae's apartment before.

"Do I ring a bell, or knock? Actually, I can't do either with these heavy boxes," Flynn hollered into a partially open bathroom window on the way to her front door.

"I'm coming, I'm coming," Jenae hopped off the couch when she heard his racket. "Hey, welcome to our flat in the sky."

"This is really nice!" Flynn's eyes scanned the main living room. "We obviously pay you too much."

"No, I don't think so."

"Where do you want me to put these boxes?"

"In here." Jenae opened the door to the guest bedroom, which served as a big walk-in closet for pharmaceutical marketing materials. She bent down to lift one.

"No, no, let me do it. It's really heavy. They over-packed these boxes. Now I know why they sent them with me and didn't mail them," Flynn said.

Flynn made himself at home on the velvet sectional couch and gazed at Hagley Park outside tall windows.

"Do you want a cup of tea?"

"Sure, just black please. No milk or sugar."

Jenae carried a tray with two cups and saucers and a teapot covered in a cozy. "I have some digestive biscuits. Let me get them."

"When was the last time you saw Fiona?" Flynn asked.

"I haven't seen her since our retreat. I haven't been feeling well. But I've been working, I promise."

"I have some bad news. Really bad news. I wanted to come tell you in person," Flynn said.

Oxygen sucked out of her lungs and the entire apartment. Her stomach knotted and she sat up straight.

"What news? Just tell me. Did you fire Fiona?" Jenae asked.

"No. I could never fire Fiona."

"Then what?" Jenae got more scared. "What? What happened?"

"She was on her bicycle this weekend on a ride near her house. It was a two-lane road with no shoulder."

"Oh no, was she hit? Is she in the hospital?"

"I don't know how to tell you this." Flynn's eyes filled with tears and his face looked mangled.

Jenae's head dropped. She braced for impact.

"Fiona was hit by a truck. She was killed instantly." Flynn made guttural exhales.

She closed her eyes, and tears ran down her cheeks, and dripping off her quivering chin onto her blouse. Jenae finally let out an exhale in convulsive cries. She took in sharp, quick breaths, and looked up as she wiped her eyes and face with the palms of her hands. No words were good enough to respond, Jenae held three fingers to her lips and stared out into the blowing tree limbs below. Her heart broke.

Flynn stayed silent in his own personal hell and looked away from Jenae. A tingling ran from his shoulders into his stomach. He took in a deep breath and sighed loudly.

"I'm so sorry. I know the two of you were very close."

"She was my best friend. She was such a good person and her life was taken just like that? She had her whole life ahead of her." Jenae struggled for breath and cried with a wail.

"Where's Neve? Will he be home soon?" Flynn asked.

"He's working in Tahiti. He won't be home for another week and a half."

"I'm going to stay here as long as you want, but is there someone you could call to be here with you when I leave?"

"Not really. I could call Helen, my mother-in-law. How did it happen again?" Jenae asked.

"She was just out on her Saturday morning bike ride getting exercise."

"Fiona loved to ride her bike."

"You know she lives out in the country a little bit off of a two-lane road. A driver just ran her over and she flew into a ditch. She was wearing a helmet, but apparently she died instantly with a broken neck." Flynn's stomach turned. "Excuse me, can I use your bathroom?"

"Sure, it's around the corner."

Jenae stood up and rummaged through a bag to find her camera. It had images of her friend inside. Memories weren't enough. Memories would fade. She didn't want to lose the memory of Fiona.

"I have to get this film developed. It's from our last retreat. We took pictures at Mt. Hutt together." Jenae squeezed her wet nose and sat at the kitchen table.

Flynn returned from the bathroom with a roll of toilet paper and set it on the table.

"Here, I couldn't find any proper tissues," Flynn said.

"Thanks. Does Gerry know?" Jenae asked. She unrolled the paper onto her hand and wiped her salty cheeks.

"Somebody from headquarters is visiting him this afternoon. I know they were dating, I'm not sure how serious they were, but I know he cared about her a lot."

"And what about her parents?"

"They called us. They're devastated as you can imagine. They're planning her funeral for Friday this week. It'll be at their hometown church in Timaru," Flynn said.

"She told me a lot about her childhood and growing up there." Jenae held her left hand on her chest as the initial shock started to wear off.

"I'll be back for the funeral. It'll be a quick turn-around, but I can drive us to the funeral if you want. There's room for Neve if he can come back early."

"Thanks Flynn."

He looked at his watch. "I'd better get going if I'm going to catch my flight. Are you going to be OK?"

"Yeah, I'll call someone if I need them, but for now I think I want to be by myself."

Flynn gave her a quick side hug and kept his head down on his walk to the elevator.

✦

The phone machine was blinking when Neve arrived back at his crash pad in Pepeete. He was high on an expectation that he nailed at least one of the two interviews he'd had with the airlines. His buddy, Dilly, had left the Air Force and was a first officer on the 737 out of Seattle. Dilly's letter of recommendation and interview prep helped Neve feel confident through the final steps toward his dream. Dilly's wife even called Neve the evening before his first interview and took him through a visualization of the process – from walking into the waiting room, to talking to the receptionist, to politely speaking to other waiting interviewees, to answering technical flying questions, and shaking hands goodbye. Neve was less stressed at the real thing having been there before – if only in his mind.

He'd be honored to work with either airline because of their great reputations. U.S. immigration had given him the green light to work for an American company. Otherwise, they wouldn't have flown him across the Pacific Ocean to talk to him. If hired, Neve learned that eventually he could commute from New Zealand, but for the first few years, it would be best to stay in the U.S. near his domicile. He had a feeling Jenae would be OK moving back home.

Her voice was measured at the beginning of the first message he played back, but ended in crying and silence. On the second message, Jenae managed to put the words together that Fiona had died, before sobbing and a click. He didn't need to listen to the rest and called her back straight away.

"Hey, I got your message. Are you all right? I'm sorry about Fiona," Neve said.

"I'm so sad. I can't stop crying."

"What happened?"

"She was hit by a truck while riding her bike on Saturday."

"Oh, God. I feel horrible. What can I do?" Neve asked.

"I don't know. It would be nice if you could come home, but I know you have to work your two weeks. The funeral is on Friday and Flynn said he would drive us down to Timaru."

"I'll have Mum check on you. And I'll check back to make sure you're OK."

"Thanks, I miss you. How did your interviews go? I'm still mad you didn't take me with you."

"I know you are. But I feel like they went well. Both airlines seem really great. Would you be willing to move back to California for training and maybe for a few years while I get situated? That's if I get the job of course."

"Twist my arm. I love my job and this country, but I'm super homesick and emotional."

"We can talk about it when and if the time comes."

"Take it easy this week. I love you."

"I love you too. Talk to you soon."

Tragedy and mixed blessings created a confusing blend of emotions in Jenae's heart. As she lay in bed, she had a flashback to when she was ten years old and her grandpa, Pappy, died. He was the first to go. She and her sister had interrupted a serious conversation in the kitchen between her parents late in the evening. Both parents cried as they talked about scheduling a flight back to Milwaukee. Everyone was in a state of shock when they learned that Pappy was dead. Jenae and her sister retreated quietly to their room and put themselves to bed.

The feeling of a pit in Jenae's stomach burned as she tried to fall asleep in a pitch-black room. Was this what it's like to die? Everything goes to black? The really dark blackness like in the bowels of a cave? To nothingness? Thoughts of a dark void terrified her. She was frozen with fear, and knew no religion to guide her on what came before or after this time on earth. Pappy was gone. It was as if he never existed; but she only existed because he had lived.

She prayed for Pappy's soul because she never had before as a child. She prayed for Fiona's soul and for Fiona's parents and sister – and for Gerry. She gave thanks for being married to her true love, and was angered that Fiona never got to experience the full life that was promised.

Chapter 28

Vulnerabilities

Logan - Jenae

I t was dusk when that old lady opened the front door. She had looked out of the window and saw a man who appeared concerned. He'd peered up into her second-floor window and around the bushes on the side of the house. One car was parked in the driveway. A blue Civic like his father-in-law drove.

"Hello? Can I help you?" Helen peeked through a four-inch opening in the door that was secured by a brass chain attached to the door frame.

"Hi ma'am. I was wondering if you could help me find a friend. I'm looking for Neve. Are you his mother?"

"Oh, yes! Are you one of his flying buddies?"

"Something like that. I knew him in California, along with Jenae. I'm just passing through."

"Oh, are you Captain Dilly? He had so many good things to say about you."

"No, no. I'm Bill." Logan shuffled his feet back and forth.

"Of course not. You'd know that he and Jenae live down by Hagley Park now. The view is amazing above the treetops from their flat. They've been there a year now already."

"Yeah, that rings a bell. What street?"

"It's on Carlton Mill Road not too far from here. In that big tall condo building. You can't miss it."

"I see. Maybe I'll stop by."

"You might wait until next week. Neve's gone for a bit. He's still working in Tahiti."

"I'll be leaving soon. When will he get back?"

"I think in a couple of weeks. Jenae wanted him to come home early. Poor thing, her best friend died in a biking accident. She wanted him to attend the funeral with her tomorrow, but he couldn't make it."

"How awful."

"Do you want to leave him a note for where you'll be staying?"

"I'm not sure of my exact address, but I'm going to check out the Bungee Adventure place near Queenstown from here. No need to bother him. I'll catch him next time I'm in town."

"Well, it was lovely meeting you. I must be off now. Good luck to you." Helen slung her pocketbook over her shoulder and locked the front door. She escorted "Bill" down the driveway and unlocked her car.

"Thanks for everything. Maybe I'll see you next time." Logan waved and slowly walked to his white hatchback.

"I'll look forward to it. Cheers!" Helen beeped her horn and sped off.

He beelined it to the tall condo on the park, but it was dark and he was hungry. It could wait until morning after a good dinner and a long sleep.

***

Jenae picked out a dark blue dress with navy pumps to wear to the funeral in Timaru. Flynn was scheduled to arrive on the early flight from Wellington, and Jenae rushed out the door to pick him up at the airport on time.

"Hey, good morning. I'm parked over there." Jenae pointed to the short-term parking lot.

"Thanks for fetching me. I can drive down from here." Flynn took the keys and tossed his backpack in the trunk of her company car. "How are you feeling this morning?"

"Ugh, I'm in a nightmare that I can't wake up from. I feel nauseated all the time. My heart is broken for me, but mostly for her family. They were so close. How about you?"

"Dealing with emotions of the family has been the most difficult. You know me, I'm just drinking a few more beers before bed to take away the sting."

"If you don't mind, I'm going to close my eyes. I've just been so exhausted. Drive carefully, OK?"

"I promise, I'll be very careful."

A two-and-half-hour nap on the road trip created a magic carpet ride in Jenae's dream. Fiona had showed up in her slumber and it made her happy. When she awoke, the pain of saying goodbye to dear Fiona made her feel sick again. She wanted to get the horrible grieving ceremony over with. There was no silver lining in her senseless death. What could the pastor say to make sense of it all?

Jenae felt in her purse to make sure she still had a sympathy card for Fiona's family. She wanted to convey the enormity of what their friendship meant to her, and words would be too hard to speak face to face.

"OK, I think we are here." Flynn drove up a hilltop and pulled into a full car park.

"Saint Mary's. Yep, this is it. Very unique architecture. Very beautiful," Jenae said.

"I think we are going to have to park on the street. There are a lot of people here already."

Edwardian Gothic styling with dark stone and white ornate outlining contrasted beautifully with the green lawn. Flynn offered Jenae his arm to steady herself as they walked up a steep hill. At the top they could see the coastline and port in one direction and snow-capped mountains behind.

"Slow down," she huffed and puffed.

"I'm keen to go into this blue door. It's closer and will save you a few steps."

They wandered into the back door and stepped into a side room that smelled of incense. A beautiful wooden casket waited patiently there. She was the guest of honor. Jenae lost her breath and balance. She grabbed Flynn's arm again and turned to talk to her friend.

"I miss you. We love you, Fiona, but I'm so mad at you. Why did you leave us?" Jenae said in a loud whisper.

Flynn tugged her arm and gently dragged her toward the back of the sanctuary. Red carpet led them to the vestibule where they signed a book and picked up a folded funeral program that read, "In Loving Memory." It had a colored picture of Fiona barefoot with a big smile on the Canterbury Coast. Jenae stopped abruptly and walked back to the greeters table and pulled the envelope from her purse and laid it in a basket next to framed pictures of Fiona.

An usher led them closer to the front where four low central posts were carved as man, lion, ox and eagle to represent the four evangelists; St. John, St. Mark, St. Matthew and St. Luke. Gerry was seated in front of them with his eyes closed. As they passed behind his pew, Flynn squeezed his shoulder. Gerry didn't move. He barely breathed.

Music quietly played from a massive pipe organ overlooking the altar. More carvings of English roses, leaves, grapes and heads of cherubs adorned choir stalls. Eight white-haired singers sat with long faces in red robes. Choir books were opened in their hands as mourners filled seats all the way to the back of the church. By the time the Archdeacon welcomed the parish, it was standing room only and some were delegated to the side porch.

Fiona's family filled the front two rows. Her father was a favorite town physician, and had treated most of the locals who had come to pay their respects to his family. The funeral director wheeled Fiona's casket in front of the altar. Cries and gasps came from the congregation. Beautiful flowers sprayed on the top of her casket couldn't assuage the sadness in the room. It was thick and stifling. Red clad choir members sang "Ave Maria" in Latin and Flynn handed Jenae a tissue from a box setting on the end of the pew. Fiona's mom was seated bent over as if her spine had melted, and her father laid his arm over her back as he stoically stared straight ahead into space.

The Archdeacon told stories of Fiona singing in the church choir, about her love of soccer and biking. He talked about the love her family shared and her successful short life. He bragged that she came to church when she was back in town to visit her folks, and remembered her volunteering at Christmas time to wrap gifts for the most-needy in their community. She was the best of Timaru.

"Fiona didn't suffer in her passing, and she isn't suffering now. She is with the Lord. Her loved ones are left here on earth to suffer, but not forever. You loved Fiona deeply. She is still loved deeply. In her short time here, Fiona gave life meaning, she was your daughter, sister, friend, co-worker, neighbor. Through suffering we find love and hope. Hope in knowing you will see her in eternity and hope that you will remember her every day on earth. We will never forget her here at Saint Mary's; she will be recorded in our sacred book of parishioners with those who have passed before her."

Amazing Grace bounced off the stained-glass windows of the church and Fiona's parents reluctantly left their beloved daughter behind. Bells tolled as the congregation slowly made their way to a reception area next door. Ladies from the church served small cakes and tea, while hugs lasted longer than usual. Gerry stood bravely amongst his coworkers but bowed out as quickly as possible after talking to Fiona's family.

The two-and-a-half-hour drive back to Christchurch signaled that the hard part was over. Jenae stared out the window. Emptiness numbed her body.

Chapter 29

Protection

Logan - Jenae

Logan milled around post boxes in the lobby until the coast was clear. An old man with big, dark sunglasses whom he'd followed through the front security door was well on his way up the elevator. Not all mailboxes had names written on the locked metal holders, but a few had envelopes visible through decorative cutouts. A janitor wearing headphones pushed a huge floor shining machine back and forth, leaving swirly patterns in his wake. He didn't see Logan hop on the elevator and hit the button for the penthouse floor. The button wouldn't light up when he tapped on it several times – it had a key hole next to it. He hit the button for the floor below it. The doors shut and the car began to rise. Two dings signaled that he'd arrived, but he wasn't sure how to proceed to figure out which apartment Jenae lived in. There were only six flats per floor. He visited the front doors of three flats on one side of the building without any clues. As he walked past the elevators again, he stopped and looked out on the trees of Hagley Park from the open-air hallway. Pine scent blew his way with a cool breeze. The next apartment he came upon had a basket set on the doormat. It was full of delicious snacks and a card that read, "Jenae."

Logan peered through a louvered bathroom window that was partially open. He carefully grabbed the bottom of one of the glass louvers and lifted it to peek inside. The louvers moved in unison.

"Ding, ding." Logan froze and watched a mom with her young son step out of the elevator. "Auntie lives this way." She turned and walked away from Logan as he leaned up against a wall out of sight.

When the coast was clear, he successfully removed all of the glass louvers from their casings and gently set them down behind the basket. "Hello? Anyone home?" He yelled into the bathroom as he hoisted himself up and over the ledge. The excitement of being a bad boy aroused him. Seeing two bras hung on the towel rack next to a closed shower curtain made it even more exciting. He knew no one was there, but he sneaked a look to make sure nobody was hiding, just for fun. Soft footsteps, toe first, led him into the hallway and he stopped at a bedroom. A comforter was heaped at the foot of the bed, and a drawer in the bedside table was open, which exposed a jewelry dish with a charm bracelet and a silver necklace. He inspected the bracelet and slipped it into his front pocket. A room full of boring boxes was next, and finally the kitchen by the front door. A framed picture of Jenae and Neve sat prominently on a radiator cover in the grand living room. He walked past it to look out the window at the view. It was beautiful, even though most of the leaves had fallen.

He smirked and picked up the wedding photo and took off the backing while making his way back to the kitchen. A tall mug with pencils, pens and a pair of scissors caught his eye. Logan carefully made two small "x's" over both of Neve's eyes in the picture and placed it back in its place. He would have stolen money if he had found any, but the most expensive thing there was a TV that would barely fit in his hatchback.

He did grab a sexy black lace bra from the bathroom after he replaced the glass louvers. He was feeling peckish and grabbed a packet of black licorice out of the basket on his way out the front door. A wave of satisfaction came over him as he walked across Carlton Mill and safely jumped into his car parked on the side of the road. *I wonder when Jenae will get home,* he thought.

——◦——

A basket of goodies with a card waited on Jenae's doorstep from Helen. Jenae grabbed a packet of chocolate covered cookies and turned on the hot water kettle before kicking her shoes off and collapsing on the couch. The note had a spring floral bouquet painted on the front. Inside it read, "Life can be wonderful and cruel at the same time. I'm sorry for the loss of your friend, please call me if you want company.

Neve will return back to you soon and the two of you will have a beautiful life together. Love, Helen P.S. A friend from America stopped by my house to find Neve. He said he knew you too." Shrills from the kettle snapped Jenae from concentrating on the note. She jumped up, hit the off switch and poured boiling water into a teacup with a tea bag and dipped it until it sank to the bottom. Punching Helen's home phone number into the receiver by memory taxed her memory. *I always forget, is it three, four or four, three?*

"Hello?" Helen answered.

"Hi Helen, it's Jenae. I called to thank you for the thoughtful basket that you left for me. I appreciate it more than you know."

"Aw, that's alright. I want you to know that we care about you. I'm sorry that your friend passed away. That wasn't fair."

"The funeral was beautiful and she'll be missed by a lot of people. I wish Neve would've gone with me, but he has our future in mind."

"He'd better get back soon. He's been away long enough," Helen said.

"I know, it's been really tough. Hopefully it'll all pay off."

"Hey, in your note you said that a friend stopped by. Who was that?"

"He said his name was Bill. He didn't give a last name."

"Huh. That doesn't sound familiar. What did he look like?"

"Uh, a white guy about your height or slightly shorter. He was wearing a knit cap, so I couldn't tell what color his hair was."

"I have no idea who he could be," Jenae said.

"He's leaving for Queenstown soon, so you may miss him all together."

"I see. Well, I'm going to eat your snacks for dinner and go to bed early. Thanks again for thinking of me."

"Good night, dear."

"Have a good evening."

The sunset was exceptionally beautiful and a newscaster on the evening news reported that particulates in the air caused the atmospheric sensation. Thousands of expatriates had been removed from the Philippines because of the super explosion of Mt. Pinatubo.

Darkness turned to pitch black and gave cover to trees in the park below. Jenae awoke and sat straight up in bed. Her sleepy wide eyes stared into the black abyss outside her window. It came to her. *The Philippines. Logan was evacuated from the Philippines.*

⸺⬦⸺

The first call of the morning was a hang up. She didn't hear heavy breathing on the other end, but got the feeling that it wasn't a wrong number. When she hung up, the phone rang again immediately.

"Who is this? Are you some kind of pervert?" Jenae yelled into the phone.

"Whoa, calm down. It's me, Neve."

"Oh, thank God!"

"Are you alright? I called to hear how the funeral went."

"Sorry, someone just called and hung up. It freaked me out. The funeral was beautiful but really sad, of course."

"Listen, I feel bad that I wasn't there for you. I should have been more supportive."

"I understand. There isn't much you can do so far away. Besides, your mum left me a nice basket when I got back."

"She's thoughtful like that."

"Hey, I'm a little concerned about something though."

"What's that?"

"Your mum said an American bloke came by her house to see you. His name was Bill."

"I don't think I know an American Bill. Who was he?"

"I'm not sure, but I'm worried that it could be Logan. Remember? He wrote that letter from the Philippines and said he was settled and you were in the clear? Well, there was a big evacuation from there because of the volcanic eruption and a few planes came here."

"Ah crap. Bloody hell."

"I just have a weird feeling about it."

"Right. I'm going to call Karl and have him come over to talk to you and Mum. You remember Karl from Honolulu, right?"

"Of course I do. He was in the police with you."

"He's on his own doing private investigations now. I'll ring him as soon as we hang up."

Helen heated a jug of water and put a pan of scones in the oven. She had written down all that she remembered from her encounter with Bill, just as Karl had instructed her to do. Jenae pulled up into the driveway first and let herself in after a quick knock.

"Hello, Helen?"

"Come on in Jenae. I'm just steeping some tea for us. Have a seat."

"Well isn't this a dodgy situation? Do you think this Bill fellow is the FBI agent that supposedly jumped off the bridge in San Francisco?"

"We know that he didn't because he wrote me a letter last year from the Philippines. And he would know your address because Neve lived with you when he applied for the visa in America. Logan confessed to me that he was responsible for holding the immigration process up for Neve because he was in love with me."

"What a diabolical creep!"

The doorbell rang and they both jumped.

"Oh dear. That must be Karl." Helen giggled and put her hand on her chest.

"Good afternoon, ladies. It's been a long time, Jenae," Karl said before kissing her cheek.

"Yes, too long. How did it work out with all of your dates in Honolulu?" Jenae gave him a hug and snickered.

"I've moved on. Should say, I settled down. I'm officially engaged to a beautiful nurse like you. Her name is Mabel."

"How exciting! I hope we get invited to the wedding!" Jenae said.

"Me too," Helen said.

"OK, let's get down to business," Karl said. "It sounds like this Logan FBI POS may have made it all the way to little old Christchurch."

"I'm not one hundred percent sure, but we hope you can find out," Jenae said.

Helen handed him a long sheet of notebook paper alongside a scone on a small plate. She served tea and talked about her notes, bullet point by bullet point. She even remembered that his temporary license plate on his white hatchback was from a dealership downtown. Jenae told Karl the story of being stalked in San Francisco, and letters she'd gotten from Logan that were forwarded to her by her ex-roommate.

"I still remember the shocking things he did in Hawaii when I was there. All under the guise of an FBI investigation. He's like a cockroach that won't die," Karl said.

"Do you want to see the letters that he sent?" Jenae asked.

"Yeah, that might be helpful," Karl said.

"I forgot to bring them. Do you want to follow me back to my flat? I have them there," Jenae said.

She beat Karl to her apartment on purpose to make her bed, clean the dishes in the sink, and swish out the toilet in case he had to use it. She grabbed a bra drying on the towel rack and looked around for her sexy black bra that she'd hung next to it. Karl walked up as she wiped the sink. He peeked through the louvered window from the breezeway.

"This isn't exactly safe, is it?" Karl moved the glass louvers back and forth. "You don't mind being watched while you sit on the loo?"

"Meet me at the front door. I'll let you in," Jenae said as she dried her hands.

So where are these letters? Jenae wandered to a closet in the second bedroom and pulled out a large manila envelope from the top shelf. Karl walked around the flat and picked up framed pictures of Jenae's family, but mostly glamour shots of her and Neve looking fabulous.

"I can't believe you ended up marrying this guy, Neve. I mean he was my best friend, but I'd never recommend him as a husband," Karl joked.

"You are one to talk, but yet you're engaged to Mabel now. How'd you manage that?"

"A lot of shiny baubles and good lovin', I suppose. Is this your wedding picture? It looks like it's in Auckland."

"Yep, a bit informal but very romantic, and efficient. The courthouse was beautiful."

"What's wrong with Neve's eyes? The picture looks scratched." Karl handed it to Jenae.

"Let me see." She touched the frame glass to wipe the smudge off, then opened the velvet backing and pulled out the picture. Her fingernails caught in grooves over Neve's eyes and she turned pale.

Karl examined the picture himself. "Somebody's got an enemy. Who's been in this flat?"

"Nobody. I mean only my work friends and Neve's family. My parents were here a while ago, but I don't think they hate him that much – you know because he dragged me halfway around the world."

"Jenae, I want you to take a look around and see if anything else is amiss."

"You know what? One of my bras is missing. It was drying in the bathroom. It was my expensive one too."

They walked into the bathroom and Karl took a look at the glass louvers. They were dusty except for two sets of fingerprints on each piece.

"What's up with this window? Did you know you can take these pieces out to clean?"

"Do you think somebody came into my apartment?"

"Keep looking. Check your closet and drawers."

Jenae looked through her underwear drawer and it all appeared normal. Her love letters from Neve were still hidden under a fresh packet of pantyhose. The bedside table drawer was open by a crack and her silver necklace was still there, but her charm bracelet was missing.

"Why would someone steal one bracelet and not take the more expensive necklace right next to it?" Jenae asked Karl.

"It seems personal. Your bra and bracelet are missing and Neve's eyes are clawed out. I'm sorry to say that if this fellow Logan is in town, he would be at the top of my suspect list."

"What do I do?"

"Stay put, and ask Helen to come over. I'm going to check out the lead from the dealership. Don't worry, I'll make sure you're safe until Neve gets back. Jesus, how did that guy manage to get a gig flying in Tahiti? Neve has the best luck."

"Thanks, Karl. Be careful. This guy is a psycho."

"I'm sure I'm a lot bigger than him and I know my way around this island better than him."

Jenae walked back into her apartment and turned back. "Remember, Helen said he was staying at a hostel downtown."

"Yep, got it." Karl didn't wait for the elevator. He two stepped down the stairwell instead.

"Fairway Motors Best Deal in Town," the billboard over a car lot filled with used cars advertised. Karl towered over the six-foot-one-inch salesman who'd sold Logan a car.

"He was here a few days ago. Paid cash. Yeah, yeah, yeah. We had trouble getting ID from him because his documents got burnt up in Mt. Pinatubo. But he was American, not Filipino – he just lived there for a while. He paid cash."

He fit the description Helen had given him and matched the make and model of car he was driving with a temporary dealer tag. Karl wandered to the hostel nearby and waited awhile outside in case a white Toyota hatchback pulled up. A hippy dippy tea shop wasn't too far away and he could watch from there, while he had a spot of tea and called his fiancée, Mabel, from the pay phone inside. Logan never showed, but the barista confirmed that he'd been a customer a few times, and was planning a trip to Queenstown to meet up with buddies at the Adventure Bungee outfit.

"Now why would anyone want to jump off of a perfectly good bridge with a bunch of elastics tied around their ankles?" Karl laughed indignantly. "Sounds dangerous."

⸻◦⸻

Helen hurried over to Jenae's condo with a small flowered suitcase and a bottle of gin and limes.

"You have tonic or soda water don't you, Jenae?"

"Yeah, yeah. It's still in the fridge from the last time that you were here."

"I'm sorry you're going through so many tough times. First your girlfriend dies and now this psycho shows up again."

"Hopefully Karl can track him down. Karl called and said he had a lead, and thought Logan had left for Queenstown."

"That would be a blessing."

"And Neve is coming home a few days early. He worked his schedule and switched with a buddy so he could work back-to-back days."

"Since you're here, do you mind if I get some fresh air before it gets dark? I haven't been on a run in a week and I need to release some stress."

"Sure honey. I'll keep the doors locked and watch out for our friend with the knit cap."

"Press 9 on the phone if you need to let anyone in at the front door."

"Got it. I may order a pizza for dinner."

<hr>

Running through mist in the middle of a winter evening was refreshing, and the beauty of a deep orange sunset filled her soul. Jenae was surprised that she could still run seven miles around the park without losing strength in her legs. She was more winded than usual. Mist turned to small droplets of rain and she lifted her breaker hoodie over her hair for protection. She reached into her fanny pack for her keychain; she must have just dropped it. She pulled a little pin light out from her nursing days and shone it on the grass around her feet. A glimmering letter "J" caught her eye and she picked it up with a sigh of relief.

Just as she crossed the walking bridge over the creek, she noticed a man sitting with his hands folded and his head down. He wore a dark beanie. Jenae shined the pin light at his face.

"Shit! Shit, shit, shit!" She ran as fast as she could to the front of her tall glowing building on the park and pulled her keys out. She fumbled to get the master key into the lock. She pressed the buzzer for her apartment building, one, two, three, a gazillion times. He came walking in a full tilt toward Jenae with his hands up.

She tried the wet keys again and again. Finally, it slipped into the groove and she got inside and slammed the door shut – seconds before he reached the threshold. Indeed, it was Logan. She turned her back to him and wanted to vomit. She tried to speak normally to one of her neighbors gathering his packages from the mailroom.

Just then the buzzer rang. Helen had finally found the number nine on the phone. Logan turned around with a shitty grin and lunged for the door handle. Jenae screamed, and grabbed the other side of the handle for a good old contest of tug of war. She put her body against the door while he jerked it with small gaps.

"Help, help. Please help me. This is a bad man." Helen kept ringing the buzzer. And Logan kept pushing. Her unknown hero dropped his packages and held the door shut by adding his strength and body weight until the buzzing stopped, and Logan walked away. Jenae made it up to her flat with her neighbor's escort.

—◆◇◆—

Logan didn't get what he wanted, but it did give him a thrill that tingled up his legs. He decided to check out of the hostel that night now that his identity was known. How could that stupid bitch, Jenae, marry Neve after all Logan had done for her. He kept his head erect and alert as he drove all night to find his friends at Adventure Bungee in Queenstown.

Chapter 30

Homecoming

Neve and Jenae

Almost six weeks away and he finally made it home to Christchurch. Some soldiers spend months, even years away from their loved ones, but Jenae didn't sign up for that. She couldn't handle the loneliness and needed support when things were good and bad. Lately, it had been really bad. Logan was nowhere to be seen and felt safest underground until he could regroup in Queenstown.

"Wait outside for a second, I have a surprise for you," Jenae said.

"I can't wait any longer. Please be quick." Neve rubbed his palms on the legs of his tight sexy jeans.

"In fact, can you run to the Chinese place around the corner and pick up a take away order? I called it in before I picked you up," Jenae asked.

"Sure, I'll be back in a flash." Neve meant it and he had the speed of a superhero especially when the reward was sexy time.

She lit candles throughout the flat and spread a container of rose petals on the floor leading to the bedroom. A bottle of massage oil sat on a towel in the shape of a heart on the center of the bed and a can of whipping cream was positioned on the bedside table.

Neve returned with boxes of food in a brown paper bag and a bouquet of fresh flowers wrapped in tissue paper. Jenae had opened a bottle of champagne and handed a glass to him after he set down his bounty on the kitchen table.

"Thank you for the flowers! I love flowers."

"You've outdone yourself. What's with the candles and the rose petals? Do you think you are going to get lucky tonight?" Neve asked jokingly with a look of delight.

"I certainly hope so, pilot Neve. She straddled him on the couch and they kissed and smooched until clothing was stretched and removed and ended up hanging on the back of the divan. He carried Jenae with her legs wrapped around his waist and half-dressed to the bedroom and forcefully cleared the oil and towel onto the carpet below. He kissed her neck and whispered everything she needed to hear to fully surrender to his passions. They spooned and laughed until hunger pangs took over and Neve smacked her ass.

"Come on. Let's eat. My tummy has been rumbling since I picked up that Kung Pao Chicken and spring rolls."

"You're not the only one. Did you make sure they put cheesy wontons in too? I'm starved."

Neve told her all about his trip to San Francisco and his interviews, as he fed Jenae bites of chicken and vegetables with wobbly chopsticks. He was told he'd hear back from the airlines by mail soon. Hiring had slowed down, but he was still hopeful. Neve asked about Fiona again, but Jenae had no more tears to cry. She needed more pillow time to process a senseless death.

"Did Karl call you and update you on the Logan situation?" Neve asked.

"He did, and I think he wants to talk to you about things. He doesn't feel like we are in any danger, especially now that you are home. But he thought it would be best if the two of you took a trip to Queenstown to track him down. According to Helen and a car salesman, that's where he said he'd be," Jenae explained.

"Logan needs to be shut down, for sure."

"To tell you the truth, I'm still terrified of the guy. Did I let you read the letters that he sent to me? I forgot to give them to Karl. Maybe you and he can read over them together and see how big a threat he is."

"I'll call him in the morning."

"I told you Logan was waiting outside of our building and tried to get in, didn't I?"

"NO, no you didn't! How was that not the first thing that came out of your mouth?"

"I didn't want you to panic."

"I'm bloody panicked all right. You've had some shitty days. I feel horrible that I haven't been here for you."

"Your mum was with me at the flat so she would have found my body eventually."

"That's not funny, Jenae. We're definitely going to track that psycho down."

⸺◆⸺

Neve walked Jenae to her car the next morning for her workday of visiting doctors. He looked around the covered parking structure and opened her door after checking the backseat.

"Pop the boot. I want to make sure nothing's in there," Neve hollered at Jenae.

"I love you!" Jenae opened her window and gave him a kiss. He looked around the car park one more time.

"I love you, too. Now roll up your window and keep your doors locked at all times."

"See you tonight!"

Her first surgery visit was quick and easy. The doctor was grabbing a cup of tea to start the morning and made time for her five-minute pitch in exchange for asthma inhaler samples. She left some pens with the receptionist along with her business card and was on her way. Five more to go and she might be home before lunch. Except every doctor's office after that had a room full of patients and stacks of magazines for her to read while she waited. Every cover had a picture of Rod Stewart and his much younger and prettier New Zealander wife, Rachel Hunter. Jenae thought back to her ten-year-old self, remembering how she and her sister would call into the radio station and request "Maggie May." It was worth waiting forty-five minutes to hear their favorite popular song. Supermodel Rachel was the most famous Kiwi at the time, except for Sir Edward Percival Hillary, who was known for exploring Antarctica. And most known for being first to summit Mount Everest with his guide, Tenzing Norgay.

On the next to last doctor's visit, Jenae ran into another sales rep who sold birth control pills.

"I heard about your colleague who got hit on her bike. I'm so sorry that she died."

"Thank you. Her funeral was on Friday, but it seems like we lost her so long ago. She's only been gone a little over a week," Jenae replied.

"If there is anything I can do, please reach out." She handed Jenae a business card.

"Actually, this may sound really off, but I haven't been feeling very well. Do you have any pregnancy tests in your bag?"

"Sure, sure. I can give you a few."

"It may be just stress, but you never know. Thanks for these," Jenae said and tucked them into her brief case.

The receptionist stood up and motioned. "The doctor can see one of you now."

"You go first. Thanks for spotting me the tests," Jenae said.

"Sure. Good luck. I hope it turns out the way you want."

What's a stakeout between friends and ex-cops? A hell of an adrenaline rush. Karl picked Neve up early Saturday morning because Neve's car may not have made it over mountain passes. Jenae's company car was the newest and most reliable vehicle in the family.

They stopped at a coffee shop near the hostel where Logan had taken up residence for the prior week. In professional detective fashion, Karl had a friendly interrogation of the barista behind the counter.

"Oh yeah, that guy came in every morning last week. He's really friendly."

"Do you know where he was going after leaving Christchurch?" Karl asked.

"Ah, yeah. He was going to hang out with friends who worked at the Adventure Bungee place near Queenstown. I had the impression that he was looking for a job."

"Did he drive a white Toyota hatchback?"

"Yeah, yeah. I sent him over to the dealership just around the corner. He got a good deal, I expect."

"Do you remember his name? Was it Logan?"

"Yeah, yeah, that's it – Logan. Like I said he was a nice guy. He wore a knit cap and asked a lot of questions like you."

"Right. Thanks for that. I'll let you get back to work." Karl raised his cup of tea in a cheers gesture.

Neve pulled out the manila envelope with letters written from Logan to Jenae. Some dated back to a year and a half ago. He handed Karl two and started reading one that mentioned Neve's name.

"I hate this piece of shit, Logan, with every fiber of my being. He promises Jenae a life of true love and happiness if she leaves me. Oh, and look here. He said he'll buy her a love bungalow on the beach for the two of them," Neve said as he held up the letter.

"Ha! This letter flat out takes credit for stopping you from getting your visa. He really screwed you. You had to come all the way back here without knowing how it'd work out with Jenae," Karl said.

"Here's the letter he posted from the Philippines six months ago. It says he got married and has changed his ways. So why is he here in New Zealand stalking Jenae again?" Neve pondered out loud.

"I guess it didn't work out with his young wife. She figured him out," Karl said.

"Come on. Let's go." Neve gathered his coat and returned his ceramic tea cup and saucer to the counter.

"Thanks a lot!" Karl waved to the barista. A bell on the door rang when he opened it into a misty breeze outside.

⸺◈⸺

Neve spread out a map on his lap while Karl blasted heat to defrost the windshield and held his hands over the blowers in the dash. They had been to Adventure Bungee in their police detective days, but Neve wanted to be sure it was the same place.

"Damn, I forgot that it's at least a six hour drive no matter which way we go. I should have rented a plane. I guess the weather would have been dicey going into Queenstown," Neve said.

"What's the plan when we catch up with this guy? Break his arm? Or make him disappear?" Karl halfway joked.

"I'm not going to jail for this guy. He's taken enough of my life away," Neve said.

"Well, I can't wait to make this guy squirm. I've got a couple of shotguns in the boot."

"Let's scare the shite out of him and maybe he'll leave the country."

"He can join the prisoner class in Australia."

They made their way to Burkes Pass and down to Lake Tekapo, while Neve filled Karl in on his flying journey.

"Jenae told me you were flying prop jobs in Tahiti. How the hell did you get that gig?"

"I made a lot of friends along the way while I was learning to fly, and everyone kind of looks out for one other. I just got back from San Fran for interviews with two big commercial airlines."

"Oh yeah, how did it go?"

"Don't want to jinx myself, but as far as I could tell it went well. I answered all of the technical questions they had for me, and I'm good to work in the U.S. now. We'll see."

"Honestly Neve, I never saw your career any higher than head bartender at the local pub. You were a disaster after you left the police."

"I guess I got on the right path. I had a lot of healing to do after the shooting."

"Alright mate. I'll give you that grace. Good on ya for putting your nose to the grindstone and getting it done," Karl said.

"So, I hear you're engaged. When is the blessed day? And more importantly, when can we meet your fiancée?"

"Mabel's great. You can meet her at the wedding if you're still around, but not beforehand. You've got too many stories on me and you might ruin it for me."

The partners in fighting crime made it into Queenstown just before dark. Neve checked them into two cheap hotel rooms on the side of the main road. Prices were economical in the off-season, which fit right into Neve's budget. After a quick shower, they headed to a local pub to grab some grub and a beer. Both ordered fish that was caught at the lake nearby with rice and veggies. Beer and good conversation counted as dessert, and they chatted up the bartender to ask about new people she'd seen in the area.

"We haven't had many visitors with such bad weather over the past month. In the winter we get the hardcore ice climbers and glacier enthusiasts mostly."

"Do you know anyone working over at Adventure Bungee?" Neve asked.

"Yeah, I do. Monro has been there a couple of years. He's a big Maori guy. Don't know if Monro is his first or last name to be honest," the bartender said.

"Do you know where he lives?" Karl asked.

"Nah, but you could probably find him at the Bungee shop next to the bridge. He runs the whole thing now. He's there year-round."

The dynamic duo gathered their jackets after three pints each and settled in at the hotel for the night.

—◆◇◆—

All the memories of defending Jenae from Logan in Honolulu came flooding back. That was when he first fell in love with his wife. He'd do anything to protect her from the menace that tried to take her from him. Neve was pissed off, and as angry as he'd ever been since Logan entered their lives. He showered, shaved, dressed and knocked on Karl's door as soon as the sun lifted above the horizon.

"It's too bloody early! I'm still dreaming and it's a bloody good one. Go away!" Karl yelled to the door.

"Finish up. I'll be back in an hour." Neve headed down the main road to a café that he'd spotted on the way into town.

Neve's life was complicated, but all he could think about was confronting Logan and forcing him out of their lives forever. He was on his own turf now and Logan wasn't going to win. He ordered a coffee with cream and sugar along with the biggest breakfast omelet on the menu. The spoon clinked against the cup as he added more sugar and stirred to dissolve it. A young waitress with her hair in a ponytail pulled a utensil set wrapped in a napkin from a pocket in her white apron and set it on the end of the table.

"I'll be back with your breakfast. I forgot, do you want toast or a biscuit with your omelet?" the waitress asked.

"Whole wheat toast will be fine, thanks." Neve smiled and nodded.

Karl followed the waitress to Neve's booth as she carried his big breakfast omelet with the grace and poise of a pageant girl.

"How'd you find me?" Neve asked as Karl sat down in the booth across the table.

"It was easy. I can find anybody."

"Can I get you a coffee or tea?" the waitress asked Karl.

"I'll have what he got. Mm . . . smells delicious. Thanks darling."

Neve waited until Karl was served coffee, then dug into his eggs and hash browns.

"Sorry, I'm starved and can't wait to get on the road to find this guy."

The waitress was no help when Karl asked about a guy with Logan's description. And the pair made their way to the local bungee spot in hopes that Monro could give them a lead.

They waited in a parking lot of Adventure Bungee in Karl's running car with the defroster on and drank coffee in white Styrofoam cups. A sign on the front door of the business showed hours open from noon to 4 PM on Sundays.

"I guess they are catering to the church crowd." Karl laughed.

"Hey, maybe you and Mabel should jump off a bridge after your wedding ceremony. It could be a symbol of a really great life together – or a really short one," Neve took the piss out of Karl.

"Do you think it's safe? I would never do it, but how do they gauge that you won't fly into the side of the bridge? Or end up in the drink?" Karl asked.

"I guess they have somebody smarter than you or me working that out."

A white hatchback drove past them and pulled behind a building that served as a souvenir and snack shop. The driver had a knit cap on and was the only occupant in the car. Karl and Neve looked at each other in surprise, and Karl reached for his ankle to check that his revolver was still in place. Neve sat up straight and cranked his head to get a better look.

"Is that him? Logan?" Karl asked.

"Shit ya, it is."

"What's the plan? It looks like he works there. Should we confront him in the store once it opens up?" Karl asked.

"You go in. He won't recognize you." Neve said.

"Right."

Chapter 31

Deja Vu

Logan and Neve

Logan unlocked the front door of Adventure Bungee souvenir shop. Monro liked to sleep in with his sheila on Sunday mornings and felt sorry for Logan when he showed up desperate for a job. He gave him a quick rundown on opening procedures for scheduling bungee jumps and running the cash register. His usual help went out of town for the weekend. How much damage could Logan do before noon?

He unlocked the front door of the store at 10:00 AM and Karl strode through it at 10:05 AM. Logan was hidden behind the counter as he bent down to replace the master key in a lock box. Karl touched a display wheel with postcards stacked neatly in silver brackets. Pictures were mostly of tiny figures hanging from a stretchy band on a bridge – the bridge outside the window and across the roadway.

Logan walked toward his first customer wearing a dark knit cap on his head. Karl caught a glimpse of his stunted scarred ear.

"Morning. Are you here to schedule a bungee jump? First jump is available at noon." Logan pointed to a sign up sheet clipped to a cork board next to the counter.

"I'm thinking about it. Where's your accent from, Canada?" Karl asked.

"Nah, I'm originally from the States, but I've been traveling in Asia for the past couple of years. Not sure what I sound like now." Logan smirked.

"Is it safe? Have you jumped off this bridge?"

"Of course it's safe. They're the first commercialized bungee jump off of a bridge in the whole world. To be honest, I just got here last week so I haven't had a chance to go yet, but I'm looking forward to it. The owner, Monro, secures everyone and makes sure it's fun and safe."

"I'm Karl, nice to meet you."

"Good to meet you too. I'm Logan."

Bingo. Confirmed and caught. A psychopath was under certain scrutiny.

"I think I'll look around for a few souvenirs while I decide." Karl patted his back pocket. "Oh damn, I left my wallet in the car. I'll be back."

"Sure thing."

❦

Rural roads butting up to foothills filled with trees and bush would hide a body for years if nobody was looking. Only a few lorries passed by while Neve waited in the car for Karl.

"It's him. He said his name is Logan."

"Are you shitting me? That was too easy," Neve said. He didn't hesitate and lifted the collar of his jacket as he walked with conviction through the muddy car park into the souvenir shop. A bell rang when the door opened, and a shadow moved in the storeroom.

"Did you find your wallet?" Logan asked his customer.

Neve stood behind a bookshelf concealing his face with an open guide book.

"What the hell are you doing in New Zealand? Still stalking my wife and scaring the shit out of my mum? We thought you were fucking fish food in San Francisco Bay," Neve shouted.

"Oh shit!" Logan lunged for a cricket bat that Monro used for sport and for protection at the store.

Neve balled his fists and took two large strides before hitting Logan's face with a left uppercut and a right-sided punch to his temple. Logan hit the floor and saw stars. He picked up the cricket bat and made contact with Neve's left knee. It buckled and he stumbled. He grabbed onto the counter top. Logan stood and ran for the back door, but found Karl blocking it with a tire iron that he'd pulled from the boot of his car. He'd considered the shotgun, but didn't want to overdo it since he was packing on his ankle already.

Blood dripped from Logan's lip onto the wooden floor as he darted for a window. He slipped through head first, but felt someone grab his legs and tug him backward. He kicked and grunted, and got a square foot punch into the bridge of Neve's nose.

"Son of a bitch!" Neve let Logan's legs go and covered his bloodied face with his hands.

"Stay here, Neve. I'll go after him." Karl walked with speed and certainty as he watched Logan use a key to open a caged fence that led to the bridge. Logan looked back at Karl, slammed the cage shut and tossed the key over the bridge and into the water below.

"You can't get me now!" Logan laughed louder and louder – until he realized that he was a caged animal unable to get out on the other side without the key.

Monro heard commotion from his cabin nearby, and watched Logan taunt his pursuers as blood ran down his face. He put on track pants and a sweatshirt and ran to the bridge in his slides. Logan stood at the jumping platform, stepped into a harness and attached a safety cord to his back. Out of listening distance Monro yelled, "don't do it Logan!"

Karl had returned back to the store and helped Neve up, and pressed a towel from a display rack against his face to stop the bleeding. They walked across the roadway in time for Logan to spread eagle and yell, "COWABUNGA!" He jumped. He jumped without attaching the bungee cord to his ankles. Crack. Logan dove head first into a pile of rocks at the bank of the river below. The river ran red and Logan was erased from the earth.

Chapter 32

Bright Future

Neve and Jenae

Queenstown police released Karl and Neve after questioning the duo, and they hurried back to Christchurch before the cops changed their minds. After Monro's statement, the police were convinced that Logan was responsible for his own death.

"He thought he could get away. I guess he forgot to attach the actual bungee cord to his ankles. If he had, he'd have easily escaped on the riverbank," Neve explained, holding an icepack on his nose.

"I can't believe it. He's finally gone. Out of our lives, forever." Jenae gently hugged his neck and pushed the button on his hospital bed to lift his head higher.

"It was him or one of us – that guy was slippery as an eel."

"Has the pain medication kicked in yet? How's your knee?" Jenae couldn't help herself from doing her own physical assessment. She wasn't his nurse, just his advocate with a lot of knowledge on how things were supposed to go. She lifted the blanket off of his knee and touched the side of his leg and then checked his pulses for circulation.

"The scan showed that my knee is fine, just bruised and swollen. The doctor should release me soon. I'm not spending the night in hospital. Can you reach in my bag and get a clean shirt for me to put on?"

<hr>

Helen waited in the parking lot outside of the condo anticipating Neve's return. She regularly worried about him when he was a young beat cop years ago, and never imagined Neve would be in a fight with a dangerous psychopath as a civilian. A mother's concern never ages out even when her children are grown. She had a basket full of scones with clarified butter and tea bags in the backseat of her car for her favorite son.

She could feel him pulling away from her and feared that he would leave New Zealand forever. Jenae had been a good force for his career and self-actualization, but Helen wished he could do it closer to home. Jenae pulled up in the circle drive with Neve in the passenger seat and Helen opened his door.

"How are you faring, son? I was so worried about you."

"I'm just fine, Mum. Nothing I haven't handled before in my boxing days. Except for my knee. I'll be limping for a while."

"I feel guilty. I told that horrible man too much information. It put you and Jenae in jeopardy." Helen hung her head and held Neve's arm as she helped him navigate his way to the front door.

"It's not your fault, Helen. He would have found us one way or another," Jenae said.

<hr>

Helen put on a kettle of water to heat and arranged her famous scones onto a plate with a knife and a small pottle of butter. Neve emerged from the bathroom freshly showered with wet hair, wearing comfortable soft sweatpants and an old worn T-shirt with rips along the neckline. His face was clean as a whistle from a shave and the only evidence of a broken nose was a nick and redness under his eyes. He expected two black eyes to settle in by morning.

After tea, Helen excused herself. Neve looked exhausted after the adrenaline wore off. He headed for bed.

"Here. Take another dose of your pain medication. It's time, and it will help you sleep through the night. And take your ice pack for your nose." Jenae handed Neve two white pills with a glass of tap water.

"I hate taking medication. These will be the only ones. I'll be fine in the morning."

"Wake me up in the middle of the night if you need anything. I think I'll stay up a bit longer and read. My mind is still racing." She tucked him into bed and kissed his cheek, although Neve would have slipped her the tongue if she wasn't careful.

She was grateful and felt blessed, but couldn't help thinking about what could have happened. The past few weeks had made her more homesick than ever and cold drizzly weather didn't help. Her vulnerability fueled emptiness and sadness inside. Her stomach turned over every time she allowed herself to think about Fiona. Jenae eventually fell asleep on the couch, before sneaking under the covers next to Neve in the middle of the night. He moaned a little when she laid her arm over his waist, but didn't waken.

Bright and early, the ringing phone woke battered Neve. He'd never rushed to answer a phone before and figured they'd call back if it was important. He brushed his teeth and stared in the mirror at his shiners. It wasn't the worst look, it actually made him feel like a badass. At least the other guy was in the morgue and Neve wasn't sitting in a jail cell. The phone rang again.

"Hello?" Neve answered it.

"Yes, this is Neve. Who am I speaking to?"

"I see. I could be available. Are you sure?"

"Alright then, I'll wait for further instruction."

"Good bye."

Neve crumbled onto the kitchen table chair next to the phone. Jenae tilted her head and squinted her eyes with skepticism when she saw the stunned look on his pale face.

"Are you all right? What's wrong?" She hunched over the table as she sat across from him.

Tears filled his eyes and one rolled down his cheek. He couldn't catch his breath to speak and just puffed out air in rapid succession. Jenae grabbed a paper towel and folded it.

"Here. What happened? Who was on the phone?"

"I got it."

"You got what?"

"I got the job. In America. With my first-choice airline."

Jenae felt her chest burst with pride and joy for her husband. She screamed.

"Oh my God! Are you serious?" She jumped out of her seat and hugged him from behind. "I'm so proud of you! What a freaking journey. You did it!"

"We did it," Neve said finally able to muster up a smile.

"No, you did it! You worked your butt off and sacrificed so much to get this opportunity."

Neve stood up and buried his face into her neck and they hugged, giggled and cried as one.

"Oh man, my mum is going to be so mad."

"Why? She helped fund your lessons all this time."

"I know. But the airline called because they want me to start in three weeks. A spot opened in a new hire class and they asked if I could fill it. They figured the offer letter wouldn't make it in time."

"It's fast, but she'll be happy for you no matter what."

"You know we are moving back to San Francisco, at least for now. I'll figure out my bid once I'm done with training. We are going back to America baby!"

<hr>

The same family and friends showed up to Helen's house that always did for special family events. Saying goodbye again was becoming a bitter sweet theme for her parties. Toasts were given and Neve promised to fly Helen out the first chance she could get there.

"You can't be too mad. You have free flights for life! Well, as long as the plane has space available seats. You even get to upgrade to first class if there's room," Neve said.

"Get a two-bedroom place, because I'll come as often as you'll let me," Helen said.

"We owe you. Come as often as you want. We could also use your help," Jenae said.

Neve looked confused and wondered what she meant. Jenae put both arms around Neve's waist and looked into his eyes and looked back at the crowd.

"Neve doesn't know what I'm going to say next but I think this is the right time to make an announcement."

"She's divorcing you!" Karl hollered from the back of the kitchen. Mabel elbowed him in the ribs.

"No, no, no. That's not it. Neve, I need to tell you that – we are going to have a baby! I'm pregnant!"

The guests cheered and it took a few beats for Neve to process the news. It was the last thing Neve expected to hear, but Helen had her suspicions. She was the first to congratulate Jenae. "I'll be happy to come and help you with my grandchild. I love babies just as much as you do."

Neve's face went pale again, but recovered when he realized that he'd have health insurance with his new job, and maybe a few dollars saved to buy a three-bedroom house.

"I'm going to be a dad! I need to sit down."

⸺⬩◉⬩⸺

Jenae gave her notice at work, which left a huge hole in the South Island sales force with both Fiona and Jenae gone. She took Flynn up on his offer to send her away with a glowing official letter of recommendation for future jobs. She would stay behind an extra two weeks while Neve finished training. The airline had sent a complimentary airline ticket for her to join him on bid day in San Francisco. Together they would embark on an unknown journey that so many had taken before. A bigger life with more adventure, greater responsibility, and certain destiny.

The End.

Also by Reggie Brick

BIG ROCK – Passion in the Pacific
BIG BAY – Fate Under the Golden Gate

Connect with Reggie:
https://linktr.ee/reggiebrick

Big Kiwi Characters

Logan – Obsessed FBI agent living in the Philippines

Jenae – Nurse and MBA graduate deeply in love with Neve, and serious about her career

Neve (AKA Neville) – Jenae's handsome fiancé from New Zealand

Bart – USAF Captain

Helen – Neve's mother

Peter – Neve's father

June Mink – Bar girl at the Eager Beaver

Joy Lyn – Logan's love interest

Niles – Jenae's older brother

Steve – Logan's bus friend

Fiona – Jenae's best friend and workmate

Flynn – Jenae's boss

Gerry – Jenae's workmate

Pepe – Joy Lyn's father

Margarita – Joy Lyn's mother

Walt – Jenae's workmate

<u>Scottie</u> – Jenae's workmate

<u>Mini Mink</u> – June Mink's daughter

<u>Karl</u> – Neve's travel buddy and good friend from the police force

<u>Mabel</u> – Karl's fiancée

<u>Deely</u> – U.S. pilot friend of Neve's